# NIGHT COLLECTOR
# JENNY CRUMB

I0553889

Martina Dalton

WRITE AS RAIN BOOKS

Cover Design by Martina Dalton
Cover Model, Madeline Dalton
*Photo by Tammy Davison*

First Edition, 2019
978-1-7331168-0-0

# Dedication

*This book is dedicated to the many people committed to bringing the arts alive in their communities. The world needs more art—whether that's visual art, theatre, dance, music, or writing. The arts have a way of connecting us and creating a place where we all belong.*

# Acknowledgements

As always, many thanks to my critique group, Writers in the Rain: Fabio Bueno, Suma Subramaniam, Eileen Riccio, Brenda Beem, and Maren Higbee for their invaluable feedback and help with this novel.

Thank you to my wonderful editor Alyssa Palmer. She is a magical person who completes her editing passes with thoughtful comments and does it at warp speed.

My family always deserves praise for putting up with my weekly absences for writing critique meetings and for being supportive of my creative endeavors.

Special thanks to my daughter, Madeline, the cover model. It's been wonderful seeing her face on each of the books! I also want to thank my son, Kai, who entertains me with interesting conversations and who gets me out of the house to watch him breakdance in competitions. My two children make me proud every day.

And last, but certainly not least, thank you to the readers who follow Jenny's journey and ask when the next book will come out. Thank you!

## Chapter 1

My parents and I had finally gotten my luggage and boxes up to my new dorm room. A trickle of sweat ran down my back. New York City was hot and sticky in the summer.

Mom sat down on the chair at my empty desk and put on a brave face, even though her upper lip was quivering. "I'm sorry, Jenny. I'm a bit emotional." Her eyes shone with tears threatening to spill. "You went to Europe for over a month this summer. I haven't had a chance to spend any time with you."

I took a deep breath and let it out slowly. "We're spending time together right now. And we just finished hauling all my stuff into the room. Let's celebrate!"

She tried to smile, but it looked more like a grimace.

I knelt down beside her chair and put my hand on her knee. "You'll see me for winter break. That's only a few months away."

She grabbed a tissue from her purse and dabbed at her nose.

"Mom, I'll be all right." I bit my lip. I hated seeing Mom upset. "NYU is my dream school. I'm in my element here."

I patted her shoulder and opened one of the boxes we'd sent here from home and took out a set of sheets. I unfolded the bottom sheet and began tucking the corners under the mattress.

"This school is so expensive." Mom stood up and helped me make the bed.

"Now, Mary." Dad squeezed her shoulder. "Jenny is well aware that she'll have to find a job to help cover expenses."

I looked up at Dad and gave him an imploring look. He shifted uncomfortably from one foot to the other and shrugged. He was doing his best to make Mom feel better, but he knew that once she got worked up, it was difficult for her to calm down.

Mom turned to us. "But we won't be able to visit you very often. We can't just drive over whenever you need something."

I pulled out my phone. "We can see each other and talk anytime we want. See?" I touched the FaceTime button and her phone rang.

She sniffled and answered it.

My face appeared on her screen. I grinned and waved.

Mom laughed and wiped the tears from her cheeks, dragging a smear of mascara across her face.

The door swung open, and I caught a glimpse of freckles and auburn curls. "Cassandra!"

In a blur of motion, I was tackled in a fierce hug.

"Hi, roomie!" She held me at arm's length. "Long time no see."

I smiled. Roomie. This was exactly what she'd said to me the very first moment I'd met her at the Sitka Fine Arts Camp in Alaska last summer. We'd been assigned as roommates, and we'd been close friends ever since.

She and my other best friend, Benny, had joined me on a month-long romp through Europe just a few weeks ago. In addition to sight-seeing, we also took down a dark entity who had tortured the spirits of women who'd been persecuted in the European witch hunts. Once we'd released the souls from the dark entity's grasp, we were able to enjoy a couple of ghost-free weeks of vacation.

"I'm so glad to see you! You're looking great!"

It was true—she was looking great. She'd held onto her freckled tan from our beach time in Europe. Her cheeks were pink and her eyes bright with happiness.

"You too!" She hugged me again and then turned to hug my parents. "Nice to see you both."

A woman with Cassandra's complexion and hair color entered the room, along with a man sporting a trimmed beard and spectacles.

"Guys, meet my mom and dad, Kristine and Liam." She motioned to her parents.

I shook Mr. and Mrs. Mackay's hands and greeted them warmly. This was the first time I'd met my friend's parents.

"So, this is the famous Jenny Crumb," her father said. "We've heard a lot about you."

I laughed. "All good, I hope?"

He gave me a curt nod. "Cassandra, we need to go. We don't want to be late to the archeology symposium." He unshouldered two large duffle bags and gave her a stiff hug.

"You can't stay even for a little while?" Cassandra's face fell. "I'd love to have dinner with you before you go."

"Sorry, sweetheart." Her mother gave her a peck on the cheek. "We're only here for one day, and your father and I are anxious to get to the lecture on the new discoveries on the Giza Plateau."

"Oh," Cassandra said in a small voice.

Her parents whisked out of the room without even a look back at their daughter.

Cassandra took a second to conceal her disappointment. "What about you two?" she asked my parents. "Are you staying for dinner?"

Mom stood up and put her arms around my friend and me. "How about if we take you girls out on the town tonight? You don't have orientation until tomorrow morning."

Cassandra perked up. "I'd love that! Maybe we can even catch a Broadway show?"

"Ooh, yes." I pulled up my Today Tix app and did a search. "There's not much available, but I see there are four tickets offered for *Waitress*. But they're in the expensive section, three rows back from stage center."

Mom bit her lip. "It's our treat. It will be fun to have one special night together before we go back home."

Dad looked a little flustered but didn't object.

The guilt of costing my parents more money than they could afford hit me hard. "Actually, I'd rather just go eat at Shake Shack and maybe catch a movie."

"Shake Shack?" Cassandra clapped her hands. "Sounds yummy!"

Dad looked relieved. "Whatever you'd like, girls."

"Now, let's get your room unpacked and set up." Mom unzipped my suitcase. "I think we have enough time to get it all done before we go to dinner."

***

The next morning, Cassandra and I were off to orientation. I attended Tisch—the performing arts division of the university, and Cassandra attended Steinhardt for studio art.

"Good luck with your orientation." Cassandra hugged me.

"You too." I had butterflies in my stomach as I watched her cross the street. It was the first time I'd been alone in this huge city with only myself to rely on.

My parents and I had said tearful goodbyes the night before. Mom had pressed something into my hand just before they left me in my dorm room. "It's pepper spray," she'd said. "Stick this in your purse and remember to have it with you always."

At the time, I thought she was being overprotective and dramatic. But now, it gave me a tiny bit of comfort knowing

4

she wanted to protect me, even though she would be all the way across the country in Seattle.

I felt a lump in my throat just thinking about them and how they were flying back to my home of eighteen years. A home I wouldn't see for four months, since Cassandra and I wouldn't be going back for Thanksgiving break.

I opened the NYU app and followed the campus map to my destination.

My phone buzzed. It was a text from my boyfriend, Mike. "All settled in?"

"Mostly," I texted back. "On my way to orientation. Call you soon."

When I arrived, there were lots of students pouring through the front door to the building. A tall woman with brown hair and glasses held the door open. "Welcome, welcome," she said. "Just head down the hall, all the way back to the auditorium. There's signage along the way."

Once inside the small auditorium, I checked in with the registrars. They sat behind a long table near the stage. I took the packet they handed me and found a seat in the second row. The room fit approximately two hundred people, and judging by the number of students coming through the door, I figured it would be filled to capacity.

While everyone got settled, I perused the schedule in my folder. My first class was Acting. It started at eight-thirty. That was pretty early, but not so early that it would require double the caffeine to get there in time.

A rustling sound snapped me out of my thoughts.

"Excuse me." A big guy stepped over my feet and sat next to me. "Sorry about that."

"No problem." I went back to reading through my schedule.

"The name's Braydon Dudek." He stuck his hand out, blocking my view of the folder in my lap.

I shook his hand. It was sweaty. "Jenny. Nice to meet you, Braydon." I looked back at my schedule and wiped my hand on my jeans.

"Where are you from?" He gave me a curious glance. "You don't look like a New Yorker."

I frowned. What did that mean? "I'm from the Seattle area."

"Seattle!" His voice boomed out. "Does it really rain there ten months out of the year?"

I smiled politely at his cliché question. "Sort of. Where are you from?" I could tell he was dying to tell me about himself.

A proud grin spread across his face. "Born and raised in upstate New York. So, if you need the inside scoop on NYC, I'm your man."

I nodded. "Nice. Thank you." I tried hard not to make eye contact with him. It would only encourage more talking.

"Let's see if we have any classes together." He snatched the schedule out of my hand and compared it to his own.

Normally, I would engage in conversation with anyone, but for some reason I knew not to with Braydon. His vibe said "needy" and "I will stick to you like glue."

"We have Acting 1 together." He poked at the line on my schedule, denting the paper.

"Awesome," I said with little enthusiasm.

"That's first thing in the morning, which is great, since I'm a morning person." He squared his shoulders and handed my now-wrinkled schedule back to me.

I ran my hand over the paper to flatten it on my notebook and quickly slipped it into my folder before he got the urge to damage it further.

"Are you a morning person?" His face was suddenly way too close to mine. "Because you look like you've got some shadows under your eyes. I'm guessing you're a night owl."

6

I groaned with barely concealed irritation. "Today, I'm not a morning person."

He snorted. "See? I was right about that. I'm usually right about those things. I'm very perceptive."

Was he perceptive enough to realize how annoyed I was?

The squeal of a microphone snapped everyone to attention.

The tall woman who'd greeted us at the entrance earlier tapped on the mic. She nodded to someone in the sound booth. "Good morning!" She pushed her glasses up on the bridge of her nose.

"Good morning!" we echoed.

The woman laughed. "I'm Caroline Isaacs. I'm the department chair for the Musical Theatre program."

The muscles in my shoulders relaxed. At least he couldn't talk to me for the rest of orientation.

## Chapter 2

I carried my iced coffee back to Washington Square and sat down on a bench near the fountain's paved circle to wait for Cassandra.

The city was in the midst of its end-of-summer heat, and I regretted wearing jeans. I pulled my cotton shirt away from my sticky back. Why was Cassandra so late getting here?

Then, I spotted two people walking at the other end of the park. A fit of raucous laughter burst out from them as they headed my way. Was that Cassandra? And who was the girl with her?

When they were halfway to my bench, I noticed the similarity between the two— Cassandra with her pale skin and her auburn curls and freckles, and her new friend with mocha-colored skin and her black curls and freckles. Their grins were identical. The girls were like bicultural twins.

"Jenny!" Cassandra hurled herself at me, knocking my latte on its side.

I snatched it up before any of the precious liquid could spill. "Hey, Cassandra." I glanced from her to her friend expectantly.

"This is April! We just met in our orientation. She's an artist too, but she does digital art, like with Photoshop. And she's from New Orleans. I've always wanted to go to New Orleans—it's such a fascinating place. The food is supposed to be to-die-for, you know? Anyway, she likes bacon too! Can you believe it? Oh, and she has a really big family with like seven brothers and sisters. I've always wanted to have siblings. She says maybe if I come visit her, I can meet some of them. We can go to the French Quarter and—"

"It's nice to meet you, April." I stuck my hand out to shake hers.

"Pleasure to meet you, too," she said.

I don't know why I expected her voice to be identical to Cassandra's, but it was completely different. Instead of Cassandra's mid-range, perky tone, April's voice was low and husky with a touch of southern drawl. Her laugh was easy and warm.

"April is coming to our room with us. She wants to see our dorm—she's not happy with her living arrangements."

"Cool." I felt just a twinge of jealousy as I watched how easily Cassandra and April interacted with one another—like they'd been friends since childhood. But wasn't that the way Cassandra acted around everyone?

I walked slightly behind them while they talked and laughed, feeling a bit like an outsider.

As we headed back to our dorm, I noticed the fountain and the big white arch that stood near the middle of the park. The closer we got to it, the more anxious I felt.

I shivered, even though the temperature was hovering just over eighty degrees. My breath quickened and grew more shallow with each step. Panic bubbled up inside me, and the distinct sensation of being enclosed in a tight space overwhelmed my senses.

"Jenny?"

I blinked. Cassandra's face was inches away from mine.

"Why are you sitting on the sidewalk?" She held her hand out to me.

From my new vantage point, I noticed passersby staring at me as they made their way through the park. My butt was firmly planted on the concrete pathway. How did I get here?

I reached out and allowed Cassandra to pull me up. "I'm... not sure."

"Are you all right?" April wore a look of concern. "Did you faint?"

Letting out a shaky breath, I responded. "I'm fine. Probably just the heat."

Cassandra gave me the side-eye but didn't comment further. I could tell she suspected some kind of psychic thing had happened to me, but for once, she kept quiet about it.

Once we were out of the park, I felt more like myself. My stomach rumbled.

"After we drop our stuff of at the room, do you guys want to go out and grab a bite to eat?" I asked.

"I'm always up for getting food." Cassandra winked at me.

"Don't I know it," I joked.

"There's a great Italian restaurant right around the corner. You okay with pasta?" April asked.

My stomach rumbled again. "Pasta is fine with me."

\*\*\*

At the restaurant, we feasted on some of the best Italian food I'd ever eaten. "God. I'm going to gain my freshman fifteen in record time."

April grinned. "Nah, it's the first week of school. We have to test out all the culinary delights that NYC has to offer. You'll work it off in class. Cassandra tells me you're a musical theatre major. You're taking dance, right?"

I nodded. "Dance, acting, and music. I can't wait to start classes."

The bill came, and I winced. From now on, I would do my best to eat in the cafeteria.

"We'll split it three ways," Cassandra said to the server.

My phone buzzed. It was Detective Coalfield. "Hang on," I said to the girls. "I need to take this."

I'd first worked with Detective Coalfield in the Seattle area when a girl from my high school had gone missing. I'd helped the police find her and was almost killed by the kidnapper in the process. Then, just a few months later, I'd helped the detective find a missing boy who'd been taken to a remote island in Alaska by his estranged father.

I pushed the accept call button. "Hello?"

"Hi, Jenny," his deep voice rumbled.

"Detective! It's so nice to hear from you," I said.

"Listen," he continued. "I ran into your dad at the grocery store this morning. He mentioned that you're going to NYU."

"Yup. Classes haven't started yet, but I'm here in the city."

"The reason I'm calling is that I just got off the phone with my old college buddy, Jeff Caruso. He's a homicide detective with the NYPD."

"Uh huh," I said, wondering what that had to do with me.

"Detective Caruso is struggling with a case that they can't seem to make headway on. When I told him about you, he said he'd like to meet with you."

I furrowed my brows. "He wants *me* to help?"

He chuckled. "A little bird told him that you had a certain skill that might come in handy. I hope it's okay that I gave him your contact info."

"It's fine. Thank you." It was nice that Detective Coalfield had faith in my ability. "I'm looking forward to meeting your friend."

"Excellent. I'm going to text you his phone number so you can have it on hand."

"That's great." My gaze shifted to Cassandra and April who came outside to join me in front of the restaurant.

"Hope it all works out. Have a great time at school, Jenny."

"Thanks, Detective." I touched the end call button.

"Detective?" Cassandra asked.

"Yeah. Remember Detective Coalfield?" I put the phone back in my pocket.

"Who could forget him?" Cassandra smiled.

April looked genuinely confused.

Cassandra laughed and linked arms with her friend. "We'll fill you in another time. Want to see our room?"

## Chapter 3

After giving April the complete tour of our dorm building, we decided to go to the new student welcome event in the park. On the way down the stairs, I caught a glimpse of a familiar face. I quickly looked down at my feet and tried to avoid eye contact.

"Hey!" Braydon Dudek shouted, his voice echoing loudly in the stairwell.

"Uh, hi."

Cassandra and April gave me a curious look.

"Jenny, right?" Braydon stopped on the stair directly below the one I stood on.

"That's me," I said in a light tone. "Sorry, we're in a bit of a hurry."

"Who are your friends?" He eyed the girls flanking my side.

"Braydon, this is April and Cassandra. Ladies, this is Braydon Dudek."

"You remembered." Braydon puffed out his chest.

How could I forget it? I tried to get around him, but he somehow made his body wider than it already was.

"Do you live in this building?" He took a bite of the sandwich in his hand, leaving a trail of crumbs from his full beard to his sweat-stained t-shirt.

13

Cassandra answered for me. "Second floor. How about you?"

"Third. There was a maintenance guy working on the elevator, so I have to take the stairs up this time." He popped the last piece of sandwich in his mouth and talked while he chewed. "Guess I could use the exercise."

"Well, it was nice seeing you, Braydon." I checked the time on my phone. "We better get going."

He stepped aside to let us pass. "See you around."

I nearly tripped on the stairs rushing to escape before he decided to join us.

Once we were outside, Cassandra gave me a funny look. "What was that all about?"

I shrugged. "I met him during orientation. He's not someone I want to be too friendly with. You know what I mean?"

April nodded. "Oh, yeah. I had him pegged before he even said a word. That guy is needy. He'll follow you around like a puppy if you let him."

"Exactly." I pointed to the booths that had just been set up in Washington Square Park near the fountain. "They're selling NYU t-shirts over there. Want to check it out?"

\*\*\*

After spending the afternoon at the welcome event, we'd gone on a long walk, exploring everything we could within walking distance of our dorm.

Hours later, with tired feet and the desire to do nothing else but lie down, Cassandra and I retired to our room to get some rest. She had achieved her goal of much-needed sleep and was sprawled across her bed, snoring.

The lights of the city drilled into my eyeballs. Groaning, I lowered the shade and covered my head with a pillow. I wondered if I would get used to the constant noise outside our windows. The muffled sounds of honking horns, sirens, and rumbling garbage trucks might become my lullabies after a while, but for now, they were keeping me awake.

I gave up any hope of sleep and grabbed my laptop from the desk. I crawled under the covers and leaned against the pillows propped up against the wall at the head of my bed. It was eleven o'clock. It was probably too late to FaceTime with Mike. I missed him.

We'd been together for over a year. He'd just transferred to Ithaca because he wanted to be closer to me. And the musical theatre program there was far better than the one he was in last year. Ideally, he would've liked to attend NYU, but he'd only made it to the wait list.

At least Ithaca was only a couple of hours away, and we could see each other on weekends.

I texted him. "You awake?"

When there was no reply, I sighed and put my laptop back on the desk.

I crawled back under the covers and tried, once again, to fall asleep.

*The girl was predictable.*

*Every morning at six—like clockwork.*

*Her long strides were pure poetry in motion. Her ponytail swung in an arc from side to side.*

*I waited behind the dumpster until she'd passed. The chloroform cloth in my hand dangled at my side as I ran to catch up.*

*She was mine.*

My eyes flew open, my heart pounding like a hammer in my chest. Great. This was all I needed to start the school year.

\*\*\*

The next morning, Cassandra and I made our way to the NYU campus bookstore to purchase our textbooks. The day was hot and muggy. The smell of exhaust, cigarette smoke, and food of questionable origin scented the air. We opened the door and stepped inside.

"Ah, air conditioning." Cassandra tilted her head back, closed her eyes and held her arms out in a salutation. "This Alaska girl does not do well in the heat."

"This Washington State girl doesn't either." I laughed. "I'm going to grab a basket." I lifted one out of the holder. "Now to check my book list." I opened the student portal on my phone.

Cassandra followed suit, and soon we'd gathered our required books. Cassandra had a bunch of art supplies, which were nearly spilling out of the basket. I had a stack of books, sheet music, and plays.

We lined up at the cash register to check out.

"That'll be $375.21," the cashier said.

I bit my lip. Good lord. That was more than my entire month's allowance from my parents. They'd even given me a little extra for books, but after yesterday's lunch and the NYU t-shirt I'd bought, I was going to be running on fumes for the rest of the month. Luckily, there were only a few days left of August. My parents would soon deposit my money for September.

I gave him my debit card and held my breath, waiting for it to clear. I relaxed when the cashier handed me the receipt and wished me a good day.

"Want to go to that bakery we saw the other day to get breakfast?" Cassandra had completely rejuvenated herself in the air-conditioned store and was bouncing on her heels.

I frowned. "I'm out of funds. Let's go dump our books in our room and head to the cafeteria. At least my meal plan is paid up."

"Okay." Cassandra opened the door, and we went back out into the slippery heat of the city.

As we walked, my insides churned. Maybe my mom had been right. NYU was one of the most expensive schools in the country. How would I afford to even get through the last few days of this month, let alone four years?

I swallowed my worry and tried to focus on how lucky I was to be here in the city of my dreams. There was so much to love about this place—theatre, the arts, the diversity of the people. But everything was so expensive.

I caught myself worrying and admonished myself for it. I needed a distraction. "The dining hall is downstairs—and we haven't even been there yet! I bet they have decent food."

She grinned. "I studied the menu they gave us at orientation. "There's a lot of local, sustainable, yadda yadda on there. But, they do have grilled cheese sandwiches and bacon, so I'm cool with that."

We unloaded our supplies in the dorm room and went down the stairs to the cafeteria. I'd decided to keep it healthy and went for oatmeal and fruit.

Cassandra was her usual self. She loaded her plate with bacon, eggs, hash browns, and toast.

Once we were seated, the dining hall began to fill up with students. A group of three girls joined us at the table.

"Where are you all from?" Cassandra asked with a mouthful of toast.

"We're both from Kansas," a girl with red hair said, pointing to her brunette friend.

"London," said the tall blonde sitting next to me.

"You're from London!" Cassandra clapped her hands. "We were just there over the summer, weren't we Jenny?"

The blonde looked pleased. "Oh, lovely. Did you like it?"

"Adored it!" Cassandra swallowed her toast and took a drink of her juice. "Except for meeting the ghost there and all. But she turned out to be a nice kid. She was just trying

17

to set the souls of women who were accused of witchcraft free… including her mother's," she said matter-of-factly.

The blonde's eyebrows shot up. "Excuse me?"

"Uh, Cassandra." I gave my friend a warning look. "Maybe they don't want to hear our stories right now." I glanced at our tablemates. "I'm Jenny—I'm from the Seattle area. My friend, Cassandra, is from Sitka, Alaska."

"You guys came from a long way!" one of the Kansas girls said.

"So did she." Cassandra pointed at the British girl with a strip of bacon. "I wish we'd spent more time in your beautiful city."

"My name is Kristina." The English girl reached across the table to shake Cassandra's hand and then the hands of the rest of us.

The redhaired Kansas girl's name was Florence, and her friend was Lola.

"Just out of curiosity," Florence asked, "what exactly did you mean when you said you'd met a ghost in London?"

My shoulders slumped. These girls would think I was crazy if I told them the story of our backpacking adventures through Europe. A dark entity had chased us from castle to castle, but in the end, evil lost to good. With the help of Archangel Michael and an army of angels, we'd defeated the evil spirit. And we'd set free the souls of thousands of women persecuted during the witch hunts.

But what should I tell them, now that Cassandra had opened her big mouth? I caught Florence's gaze and instantly knew she wouldn't judge me. There was just something about her that said she was open to what we had to say.

I cleared my throat. "I guess you could say that I have a flair for the paranormal."

Florence cocked her head to the side. "Huh?"

I met the gaze of everyone, including Cassandra. "I'm psychic."

Florence gasped. "That is so cool."

Her friend Lola looked skeptical. "Yeah, right."

"No! She is." Cassandra leaned forward. "You won't believe all the stuff she can see and sense. It's amazing."

Lola smirked. "Okay, if you're so psychic, tell me something about *me* that nobody else knows."

I gave a nervous laugh. "It doesn't always work that way. I can't force it. It just happens—but not always."

Lola's smug expression said it all. "Right."

I took a breath. I wasn't used to people not believing me. Most of my friends had accepted my gift. I zeroed in on Lola—her dark hair and big brown eyes. I let my focus diffuse, so I was aware of her, but not the details. Just her aura and the person she was at her core.

Images began to slide into place, starting with a person who wanted to connect with Lola. "Who is the grandmotherly person behind you?" I asked. "She's short and round—dark curly hair, but with streaks of gray."

Lola frowned. "I have a grandmother who passed, but most kids our age have at least one grandparent who's passed."

I listened to the woman behind Lola for a moment and then laughed. "Your grandma has a sense of humor. She says she can't believe you got into NYU with your grades."

Lola's face reddened. "Again. That could apply to lots of people. And my grades were fine."

Florence gave Lola a sideways glance and raised her eyebrows but kept quiet.

"Give me your hand," I said.

Reluctantly, Lola reached across the table and let me grasp her hand.

The pictures came in rapid succession. A little girl growing up with a big family. School, ballet, music. I watched her zip through the years. Dance recitals, lots of them.

"You're a dancer," I said.

19

Lola rolled her eyes. "So? A lot of people at NYU are dancers."

"Your grandma sat in the front row for every single dance recital. She was your biggest cheerleader."

Florence gaped, open-mouthed. "You're right. Her grandma came to every one of her performances."

The vision continued. I saw Lola struggling to keep her weight down. Ballet dancers were so thin. "You're not eating enough, so you're going into starvation mode. Your body is having a difficult time sustaining its energy level because you're so active. You're tired a lot."

Lola's hand tensed in mine. She stared down at the diet soda and salad with no dressing in front of her.

Not wanting to be too harsh, I added, "But you're incredibly talented. Your dream is to dance with the Metropolitan Ballet—and I see you achieving your goal if you take care of yourself. You're a beautiful dancer. You'll be noticed."

Florence practically fell off her chair. "Everything Jenny said is true. This is unreal! Do you do readings? Will you do mine? I'm willing to pay."

"Me too," Kristina said. "I'd love to have a reading. How much do you charge?"

I was taken aback. They were willing to pay me for a reading?

When I was silent a beat too long, Cassandra said, "She charges twenty-five dollars for a half-hour reading. Normally, she charges more, but college kids are poor, so she has a special rate for students. Isn't that right, Jenny?"

I felt myself nodding. "That's right."

"Come by our room tonight if you want the reading in a more private setting." She gazed around the dining hall. "You don't want all these people overhearing what she has to tell you."

"I can stop by tonight," Kristina said eagerly.

"Same here," Florence said. "What time? Where's your room?"

Cassandra pointed at Kristina. "You can come up at six-thirty. We live in this building. Room 202." Then she turned to Florence. "Want to do your session after hers?"

"Sure. I don't have anything else going on tonight."

"Great!" Cassandra said. "Lola, what about you?"

Lola's mouth was set in a tight line. "No, thank you."

Cassandra shrugged. "Okay. Then, it's all settled. See you two this evening." She motioned toward Kristina and Florence.

I had no idea Cassandra was such a hustler.

Lola stood up, her shoulders stiff. She took her tray and headed toward the garbage cans.

"Wait," I said while Lola was still within earshot. "If you don't mind, could you guys keep this quiet?"

Kristina blinked. "You mean, don't tell anyone else about our readings?"

Oh, good. They understood. "Yes, thank you."

"May I ask why?" Kristina's brows furrowed. "Don't you want to make some extra cash?"

I squirmed in my chair. "I do, but I don't want a bunch of people to know about, you know…"

Cassandra giggled. "Oh, Jenny, you are way too modest. If I had your gift, I'd be shouting it from the rooftops."

The horror of that image gripped my chest and squeezed. I just wanted to focus on school and hone my skills as an actress—not as a psychic.

Kristina shrugged. "If you don't want anyone to know, that's okay with me. We'll keep it quiet."

I breathed a little sigh of relief. Crisis averted. For now.

# Chapter 4

Aside from the butterflies fluttering inside my rib cage, I was a tiny bit excited to earn some extra money.

But how exactly did one go about giving a reading? The one I'd done for Lola at breakfast hadn't gone well. She'd seemed closed off and unwilling to acknowledge anything I'd told her. Was I *that* wrong about her life or was she just skeptical of psychics in general?

I grabbed my phone and was about to call my mentor, Celine, when I realized it was much earlier back in Seattle. She might still be sleeping.

Instead, I turned on my laptop and googled how to do a psychic reading. After scrolling through several pages of advice, I came to some conclusions. I needed to put protections in place to shield myself from other people's troubles through prayer and mantras. I needed to not censor myself, even if the information I got didn't make sense. And I needed to avoid judging others for their past mistakes. Another important point was to not lead them down a path I thought was appropriate for them. That would be for them to determine. I could only be the messenger or conduit of information.

I read a bit more about the atmosphere and environment you could create with incense or candles... but we weren't allowed to have that kind of stuff in the dorm rooms. I thought if I turned off the overhead ceiling lights and just turned on my desk lamp, it would help to create a cozier feeling. That would have to do for now.

Maybe if I ended up doing a few more readings, I would look for some other ways to create a calm environment, despite the noise from the city outside the window.

Cassandra burst through the door. "Look what I found!" She held out her hand. In her palm were crystals of various shapes, sizes, and colors. "Most of them are quartz. I got them from a guy I met who's a geology major."

My jaw dropped. "You are a mind reader!"

"Huh?" Cassandra put her free hand on her hip.

"Our room doesn't look like a place for psychic readings. I was worried that it didn't have the right energy."

Cassandra laughed. "Oh! That's kind of funny." She grabbed my hand and poured the chunky crystals into it. "I have a pretty dish you can put these in."

"Thanks," I said. I watched her dig around in a box stashed under her bed. She unearthed a glass dish with a floral design stamped on it. "Here."

I poured the crystals into the little dish. The light reflected off each surface and made the colors dance. "Beautiful. This is perfect. Thanks, Cassandra."

She smiled. "No problem. You can push this ottoman between both our desk chairs, like a little table, and set the dish in the middle."

I grinned. "You're pretty awesome, you know that?" I stood up and hugged her. "Thank you."

She pulled away and a look of determination crossed her face. "Let's tidy up the room before Kristina and Florence come over."

\*\*\*

I didn't know where the time had gone, but it was now a few minutes before six-thirty. My palms were sweating. My nerves were getting the better of me.

I'd spent the last two hours centering myself and saying the protective mantras that Celine had taught me. I was ready—but terrified.

Cassandra reached into our mini fridge and pulled out two bottles of water. She set them on my desk. "For you and your first client."

I swallowed. "My first client. God. That sounds weird."

A knock on the door sent my heart into my throat.

"That will be Kristina." Cassandra opened the door. "Welcome! Why don't you have a seat?" She gestured toward the chair opposite me. "I'm going to go study in the cafeteria." She grabbed her backpack from her bed and winked at me. "See you in a while."

Kristina sat down and gave me a nervous smile. "I've never had a reading before. This is exciting."

Her English accent sounded so formal, it got me even more nervous than before. Somehow, I felt like a fraud. Like I was an actress pretending to be a psychic. My mouth went dry. I reached for the bottles of water Cassandra had placed on my desk. "Water?" I handed her a bottle.

She cleared her throat. "Yes, please."

I took a big sip and savored the coolness trickling down my throat. I took a deep breath and let it out slowly. "I have a confession to make."

Kristina raised her eyebrows. "You do?"

I took another sip of water. "This is the first time I've done a formal reading for anyone."

"Really?" She tried to smile, but it faltered.

"I'm sorry. Did I make you nervous?" I bit my lip. "I should say, it's not the first time I've done psychic work— I've helped the police find missing people and..."

"No, no, it's fine," Kristina stammered. "I'm just not sure what to expect, that's all."

I realized it was my job to put her at ease, not to make her anxious. "First, I'll just sit for a few minutes in silence."

A taxi honked outside. Someone yelled a profanity, and another, more insistent, honk sounded. Great.

Kristina's laugh had a tremor in it. "Ha! Silence. Funny."

I smiled. "As silent as possible, anyway. Then, I'll focus on your energy. Is there any particular issue you want me to hone in on or do you just want a general reading?"

Kristina shrugged. "Just a general one, I suppose."

"Okay, that's fine." I closed my eyes and breathed deeply for a few minutes, letting my body settle into Kristina's energy.

I opened my eyes and the images began filling my head. I let them out in words, trying my best to not edit what I saw. "Your parents are still living in the UK, right?"

She nodded.

I smiled. "You have a little sister. She's blonde like you."

"Yes," Kristina answered.

"It's funny because she's watching everything you do and wants to follow right in your footsteps."

Kristina laughed. "True."

I saw Kristina in a theatre. She was wearing black and was rushing to and fro, backstage and then into the sound booth. "Are you a stage manager?"

Her eyebrows arched. "Yes."

"Is that your major?"

"I have a double major. Stage management and also sound engineering." She shook her head. "This is incredible."

"You're really good at both," I said.

The images changed, and this time, I saw Kristina in her dorm room. Her roommate was on her bed, scowling, headphones plugged in. She made a sour face as Kristina

25

said something to her. "Are you having issues with your roommate?"

Kristina gasped. "Yes."

The image of the roommate twisted. Her face was ugly, but not because of her looks, but because of what was inside her. I saw constant struggles for this girl. Struggles to get along with others, struggles to make and maintain friendships. She was sour. The negativity poured off her.

"Are you and your roommate not speaking to each other?" I asked.

"Well, we've only known each other for a few days, but we don't seem to communicate much. When she does talk to me, she's not very nice."

I wanted to tell her to stay away from this girl. But, that wasn't my place. Instead, I said, "If you need to switch rooms, the housing number is on the NYU website."

"I've considered it." Kristina shifted uncomfortably. "I've thought about sending a message to my RA."

"That's a good idea. Go with your gut instinct."

"Hmm. Okay. My gut is telling me I don't want to room with her." She laughed nervously. "It's been a bad start to the year," she said.

"I can see why." I took a sip of my water. "But just know that it isn't you. She's struggling and might take it out on anyone close to her."

Kristina frowned. "That's sad."

"It is. But maybe it will work out for the best."

Kristina nodded.

I changed gears. "As far as that boy you're interested in? The one you met during orientation?"

She gasped. "How did you...?"

I smiled. "He's interested in you, too. He's a nice guy."

The minutes flew by. I found that I enjoyed telling her information that might be helpful to her in the future.

Before I knew it, the timer on my phone beeped. "I guess our time is up."

"Thank you very much," Kristina gushed. "This was amazing. *You're* amazing. Thank you." She dug in her pocket and pulled out some money. "Twenty-five, right?" I nodded but felt a pang of guilt. Was it wrong to expect money for helping people?

"That peace of mind,'" she said, "especially that bit about my roommate—was worth every penny. Thank you." I took the money and hugged her. "You're welcome. I hope it all works out."

When she slipped out the door, I called. "Just leave it open. Florence should be here any minute now."

While I waited for the next client, I saw Braydon Dudek shuffling down the hall. He stopped when he saw me staring. "Oh, hey, Jenny." He came back to stand just inside my room. "Nice place."

Florence would be here any second, and I didn't want Braydon to grill her about why she was visiting. "Thanks. I have a friend coming over any minute, so I guess I'll see you around."

A look of disappointment crossed his features, but was gone so quickly, I barely had to time to recognize it as that. He shrugged. "Okay. See you in class tomorrow."

I'd almost forgotten. All the more reason for me to shoo him out as soon as possible. I'd be spending enough time with him already. "See you bright and early, then."

"Indeed," he said. He turned to leave just as Florence arrived.

I got up from my chair and rushed to greet her. "Hi, Florence! Come on in." I closed the door before Braydon could engage.

"Have a seat." I motioned to the chair formerly occupied by Kristina. "Let's get started."

\*\*\*

27

I'd made fifty dollars! It wasn't going to pay for tuition or room and board, but it definitely made me feel better. A steady part-time job would be ideal, but I couldn't commit to one until I knew how demanding my school schedule would be.

Unfortunately, all the on-campus jobs were taken by work-study students. I had only qualified for two hours of work-study per week. With the minimum wage being just over ten dollars an hour, it didn't seem worth the effort.

I leaned back on my pillows and sighed. If I took too many readings, people would catch on to my gift, and I didn't know what they'd think about me. Also, I'd probably have to get a business license.

Cassandra entered the room, her face flushed from her climb up the stairs. "Well, how did it go?"

I grinned. "Really well. Both Kristina and Florence were happy with their readings."

She sat on my bed next to me. "Should I put the word out that you're ready for business?"

"No!" I said a little too quickly. "I mean, let's just take it slow. I'm not sure I want many people to know I'm a psychic." Just saying the word "psychic" out loud made me feel weird.

"Why not?" Cassandra wrinkled her brow. "It's such a cool ability."

"You're right, it is... but I don't want to be a freak show. I'd rather wait for people to get to know me before they find out what I can do."

Cassandra was quiet for a moment. "Okay, Jenny, if that's what you want." She got up and started rummaging around in her dresser.

Had I hurt her feelings somehow? I knew she was just trying to help me. "What're you doing?"

"Picking out what I'm going to wear for the first day of school tomorrow. Did you hear that the temperature is going to drop back down into the seventies? I'm so tired of being hot. I'm looking forward to some mild temperatures."

She seemed to have gotten over whatever was bothering her. "So am I." I checked my weather app. "Looks like the high will be around seventy-five tomorrow. That's perfect."

Cassandra pulled out a green, short-sleeved shirt and paired it with white, cropped pants. "This will be cute—and I can't wear white after Labor Day, so I better get as much wear out of these while I can. September's right around the corner."

My phone buzzed. "It's Mike!" I squealed. I hadn't heard from him since he got to Ithaca.

I read his message. "Sorry, I didn't see your text earlier. Arrived late at night and crashed. Been setting up my dorm room. Have you started classes yet?"

I'd forgotten that Mike would have to live on campus. He was technically a sophomore, but all musical theatre students transferring from one school to another had to enter in as freshmen, even if they'd had training elsewhere.

"Classes start tomorrow. How about you?" I texted.

"Day after tomorrow on Thursday."

"Want to FaceTime?"

"I'm headed off to an event for the theatre department," he texted. "How about after classes tomorrow night?"

"Sounds good. Talk to you soon. Love you." I set my phone down.

The screen lit up with another message. "Love you too."

I smiled, even though he couldn't see me. That old saying about being apart made the heart grow fonder was true for me. I hadn't had a chance to see much of Mike during the summer, so I was eager to meet up with him in the next few weeks. We'd agreed that he would come to the city for our first visit. We'd catch a Broadway show or two

29

and spend some time getting comfortable with each other again.

Cassandra interrupted my thoughts. "I just talked to Duncan." She threw herself down on her bed and squeezed the stuffed bear propped up on the pillows. "It's morning in the U.K. He's flying over during Thanksgiving break!"

"That's awesome. Mike will be here too. It's too expensive to go home for less than a week."

"We can double date for part of it." Cassandra grinned. "It's going to be so much fun."

As I got ready for bed, my mind wandered to walks in Central Park, eating out in Times Square, and exploring Little Italy and Chinatown. This was going to be a great year.

I drifted off to sleep the moment my head hit the pillow.

*The woman hadn't changed her routine yet. She ordered the same thing every morning. A large coffee with cream and an egg breakfast sandwich.*

*Today, her routine was about to change.*

*My van idled in the delivery loading zone.*

*I got out as she exited the shop.*

*"Excuse me, ma'am. You dropped something."*

*She fell for it, just as I knew she would.*

*She was stronger than I expected.*

*But she was mine.*

I sat up, my blankets twisted around my legs, my pulse racing. What the hell? I couldn't go down this rabbit hole while going to school. Even if I did, I had no idea what was going on. Was I inside the head of a kidnapper?

Cassandra's alarm went off.

She opened her eyes, turned off her alarm, and literally bounced out of bed. "Happy first day of college!"

I put my hand to my heart and let the pace of it slow.

My friend turned to look at me. "Jenny, what's wrong?"

30

"Bad dream. It's okay." I swung my legs onto the floor.

"Was it a vision?" Cassandra dropped the armful of clothes on her bed and sat down next to me.

"I guess so. But I have no idea what it means." I described the dream in detail.

Cassandra's brows furrowed. "This sounds serious. Shouldn't you call the police?"

I shook my head. "They'd just think I'm crazy. Besides, I don't have any details for them. I can't tell them who the man is. I don't have a license plate number of the van he was driving. I barely have a description of the woman he kidnapped."

"What do you remember about her?" Cassandra grabbed a notebook and a pen from my desk.

I closed my eyes and tried to visualize the scene from my dream. The woman came out of the shop. "She was wearing a skirt and a white blouse. Medium height. Darkish hair. I don't know."

Cassandra shook her head. "That could be anybody. Anything unusual about her?"

"No. She was just an average woman. Like you said, she could be anybody."

"I guess you can't call the police yet." She paused. "Have you talked to the guy Detective Coalfield told you about? The one with the NYPD?"

"No. Not yet. I kind of forgot about it until now, to tell you the truth."

"If you get any more details in your next dream, maybe you should consider telling him." Cassandra got up and gathered her clothes. "I'm going to hit the shower. My first class starts in an hour." She opened the door and headed down the hall toward the bathroom.

"Yeah, I better get ready too."

# Chapter 5

The short first week of school went by quickly. It was Friday, and I was ready for the weekend. There was already so much information I needed to absorb—and there'd only been three days of class.

I had to memorize lines from three separate scenes, learn two songs and a dance routine by Monday.

Apparently, this was the professors' way to find out what we could do under extreme pressure. I wondered how many of us would cave and lose our minds.

I stopped on the way to pick up my mail and then headed to my room.

Cassandra was already there, draped across her bed. She'd propped a book up on a pillow and was deeply immersed in reading. Her head popped up as I entered. "Hey! Where've you been? I thought your last class ended at three."

I held up my mail. "I forgot to pick up my mail yesterday, so I thought I'd grab it before the weekend." I had a letter from Mom and Dad and something from the university. I opened the one from NYU first. As I read, I could feel anxiety building inside me. "Oh, my God." I swallowed hard. "It's a bill for two thousand dollars."

Cassandra set her book down. "I got one of those yesterday. Something about student activity fees and some other random stuff. I just let my parents know. They said they'd take care of it."

My heart sank. My parents were already strapped with a huge portion of my hefty tuition. I couldn't ask them for more. I bit my lip and opened the letter from my family.

"Dear Jenny," it read. "Hope you are having fun during your first week of school! Just wanted you to know that we deposited September's money a little earlier than normal, since you probably had a few unexpected costs. We put $350 into your account. Don't spend it all in one place! Love, Mom and Dad."

I closed my eyes and sighed. How was I going to tell them I needed $2,000? I looked at the due date—September 18th. My stomach churned. "Cassandra, do you know some other people who might want readings?" Maybe I could call the financial office and pay in installments.

She perked up. "Sure! I could ask my whole department."

"No," I blurted. "Don't spread the word—just mention it to a *few* people to see if they're interested." Even though NYU was a huge school, talk would still spread to the musical theatre department. I didn't want that.

"Sure. I'll round up a few more people—until you tell me when you're ready for more."

"Thanks." I let out a big breath. "That would be great."

"Want to go to a movie with April and me tonight? We want to see the new one with Liam Hemsworth. He's so yummy."

I thought about my soon-to-be empty wallet. "No, that's okay. You two have fun, though."

"Oh, come on. It's my treat." She gave me the puppy dog eyes and prayer-hands thing.

I hesitated. I'd always had a problem with pride. But my friend was being so kind, and I didn't want to turn her

33

down because of my own hang-ups over money. "Are you sure? I can pay you back later."

"No, you can't. I insist. It's my treat. Really." Cassandra gave me a warm smile. "Let's go downstairs and get dinner before we go. We have to meet April in Wasquapa at six. The show starts at seven, and we need time to figure out which subway to take."

I wrinkled my nose. "Wasquapa? Sounds like a town in the Pacific Northwest."

She laughed. "No, it's short for Washington Square Park. I learned that people will automatically know you're not a local if you don't use the nickname."

"But we *aren't* local," I said.

"We will be, though." She grabbed my hoodie and handed it to me. "And we don't want anyone to think we're noobs. Come on. Let's go."

I followed her out the door. Even Cassandra cared what other people thought of her sometimes.

***

When the movie got out, the three of us flowed out into the street with the rest of the crowd.

The evening was cooler than I'd anticipated. The wind whistled through the streets like it was racing through a canyon. Our hair flew around our faces. I zipped up my hoodie and wrapped my arms around myself.

I reached into my jeans pocket and pulled out the hair tie I'd stuffed in there earlier. With a well-practiced motion, I wrangled my long hair into a messy ponytail to keep it from getting more tangled.

"Brrr." Cassandra tugged her jacket down around her hips. "I just got used to the heat. Why did it have to get so cold all of a sudden?"

April shivered and rubbed her hands together. "You two should be used to the cold where you're from. I grew up in New Orleans. I'm literally freezing!"

"Speaking of New Orleans," Cassandra said, "I'd really love to visit there one day."

April's face broke into a smile. "Why don't you all come over for spring break? You can stay with my family. We have a big house, and we'd love to have you as guests."

While Cassandra and chatted about the trip, a pang of sadness came over me. I wasn't sure I'd be able to afford the flight home, let alone take a vacation during spring break. Even if I found a job, I didn't think that my parents would be excited about me spending money on a trip—especially since I'd spent a lot in Europe over the summer.

As we got closer to Washington Square Park, a bright barb of lightening lit the sky, followed by a boom of thunder.

People scattered to find shelter.

"A thunderstorm?" Cassandra began running. "We better get inside before the rain starts to fall."

"Rain is one thing, but more importantly, we don't want to get hit by lightning!" April shouted while she tore after Cassandra.

There was no way I was going to get left behind. I ran as fast as I could to catch up.

The leaves on the trees vibrated with the motion of the wind. An eerie feeling came over me. Something was about to happen.

Another flash of lightning illuminated the sky. I stared ahead at the massive tree standing on one side of the park. A body hung from the neck in one of the lower branches.

It was a woman.

She swayed back and forth with the gusts of wind, her long skirt fluttering around her ankles.

Horror gripped my chest. "Stop!" I shouted at my friends.

They ceased their frantic journey and turned to look at me. I pointed to the tree. Another flash lit up the sky. The tree was transformed from a gothic silhouette in the dark to a glowing beacon of light and energy. The woman was still there—hanging by her neck. She was African American. Her dress looked like something from the olden days. An apron was tied around her middle.

Rain burst out of the heavy clouds racing overhead in the dark sky.

Cassandra's pale face dripped with water. "Is that?"

"A body?" April finished her sentence, her eyes wide.

Rain ran in rivers from my hair and shoulders. "I'm afraid so."

We hesitantly approached the tree. My stomach roiled. What kind of a sick hate crime was this, anyway?

"We should call the police!" Cassandra shouted over the howling of the wind.

The steady downpour of rain made that option impossible. "No. Our phones will short out with all this water. Let's wait until we get back to the dorm."

We inched forward, trembling from the cold and fear of getting closer to the body. Finally, we arrived near the area we knew she'd be hanging.

A flash of lightning brightened the sky, making my teeth vibrate from the electricity and subsequent boom of thunder.

The tree lit up once again.

The body was gone.

# Chapter 6

We stood, dripping, in our dorm room. A puddle the size of a small lake pooled at our feet. I grabbed clean towels from the storage cube next to my bed. "Here. Dry off. I'll turn on the heat." I toweled off and twisted the dial on the old-fashioned radiator.

"There was a woman hanging in a tree—*dead*." April gestured toward the window facing the park. "And then a second later, she was gone." She shook her head, spraying water droplets everywhere.

I bit my lip. "I know."

"I'm freaking out." April was visibly shaken. "I swear to God, that was the weirdest thing I've ever seen." April ran her hand over her wet face. She flipped her head upside down and wrapped her hair in the towel.

Cassandra smiled. "I can safely say that's *not* the weirdest thing that I've ever seen. If you hang around Jenny long enough, you'll see plenty of weird stuff."

My mind began the process of trying to decipher why we had seen the ghost. "Any ideas about who that woman was?"

"Nope. I got nothing," Cassandra said. "She was wearing a long dress, so maybe a ghost from the turn of the century or thereabouts?"

April stood up straight and scrutinized me. "So, you guys never told me what the deal is with you. You hinted, but I'm guessing you've got some kind of a supernatural thing going on. Am I right?"

Cassandra looked at me, anxious to get permission to tell my secret. I nodded.

"Jenny can see dead people," she said with an air of importance.

"Sorry for stating the obvious, but didn't we *all* see the dead woman hanging in the tree?" April moved to stand in front of the radiator with her arms out, letting the heat circulate around her.

I laughed. She was right. All three of us *had* seen the woman.

"But Jenny is psychic!" Cassandra continued. "I mean, really psychic. Like, she can see and talk to ghosts, fight dark entities, converse with angels—the works."

April crinkled her nose. "Fight dark entities? What?"

"It's a long story." Cassandra went to stand next to her friend by the heater. "Or rather, *stories*. Plural. Let me tell you—after meeting Jenny, I've been drawn into her world. And because of that," she began ticking points off on her fingers, "we found a missing boy, found the dead body of our friend's cousin, stopped a malevolent ghost from hurting people at a theatre, and helped release the souls of women persecuted in European witch hunts." She thought for a moment. "That's where the angel part comes in, by the way. We couldn't have saved the women's souls if Archangel Michael hadn't stepped in to help."

April's mouth hung open. "You're kidding, right?"

Cassandra and I were silent.

"You're not kidding." April furrowed her brows. "So, you're delusional, then."

I shrugged. "You can choose to believe whatever you want."

Cassandra was not about to let it go. "It's true! I only told you a fraction of what we've encountered. And it's all due to Jenny's gift."

"I think you guys are awesome, but if you expect me to buy into this, I really need some proof." April lowered her arms to her sides. "I'm not a big believer in the woo-woo spirit world. It reminds me of all that voodoo crap in New Orleans. Fun for the tourists, but it's staged. Now, the ghost thing seemed real. I saw the lady hanging in the tree with my own eyes, same as you."

I seriously hated it when people asked me to prove that I had psychic ability. I wasn't a sideshow act. I'd only been here for a week, and already I'd been challenged to prove myself—twice.

"Show her, Jenny." Cassandra put her hands on her hips.

I scowled at April.

She blew out a breath. "I'm sorry if I offended you. I'm a skeptic, but I'm willing to believe if I have proof."

I glanced at April and spotted a bracelet on her wrist. It looked like it might have been carved out of bone and was brownish in color.

"Hand me that bracelet." I pointed to her wrist. "And don't tell me anything about it."

Her eyebrows rose. "Why?"

"Just hand it to me. You'll see." I reached for the bracelet as she held it out. I closed my eyes. Images began playing on the screen behind my eyelids. Not just images but smells and sounds too.

*Flash.*

*I stood in the grasslands, the warm, dry wind blowing my curls away from my face. The smell of sun-baked dirt swirled around me. I looked over my shoulder and caught a glimpse of my village, partially hidden by trees and tall bushes.*

*Children were playing a game of tag around the well. I spied one of my own, practicing his skills with a spear next to the old acacia tree. "Gathii! Be careful!" I shouted at him.*

*He turned and grinned. "I am being careful, Mama."*

*My little girl came running straight at me, bare feet flying over the soft earth.*

*"Slow down, child." I caught her in my arms and whirled her around. "Aluna, you are getting so big. And heavy."*

*Aluna fingered the bracelet on my wrist.*

*"You love this bracelet, don't you, child?"*

*Aluna nodded as she twirled it around my arm.*

*"Someday, it will be yours."*

I opened my eyes. "The bracelet is old."

April nodded. "That's obvious."

"Are your ancestors from Africa?" I ran my fingers over the worn carvings in the bone one more time before handing it back to her.

She tilted her head to the side. "Also obvious. I'm African American, so… yes."

"Do you know any of your ancestors' names? Or where in Africa they came from? Because, as I held your bracelet, I was suddenly transported there. The scenery looked a bit like Kenya—at least, from what I've seen on television."

April stared at me, her expression unreadable.

"I saw a woman. She had two children. A boy named Gathii and a girl named Aluna." I shifted my weight. What if I'd gotten this all wrong? Anxiety began creeping its way into my chest.

"Aluna?" April's eyebrows rose. "I had a great-great grandmother by that name. We don't have a good record of our family history, but that name is one I know. It's my middle name. And my mom's middle name, too."

Relief washed over me. "So, I did connect with your ancestors, then."

April shrugged. "Maybe."

I desperately wanted to roll my eyes, but I held back.

Cassandra wasn't so diplomatic. "Are you serious, April? She just identified the name of your great-great grandmother. You still don't believe her?"

April smiled. "Possibly—I mean, I believe her a little more than I did five minutes ago."

Cassandra groaned. "Wow. Tough customer." She pulled on a dry hoodie and fluffed her auburn curls. "I'm craving cookies. Let's go see what's left in the vending machine downstairs."

On our way to get cookies, a petite girl who lived a few doors down the hall stopped us. "You're Jenny, right?"

I hesitated. "Yes. And you're?"

"Mila." She smiled. She ran her fingers through her pixie-cut hair. "I heard you do readings. I'd love to schedule one."

"She's available for a reading tomorrow morning at eleven o'clock." Cassandra winked.

"Oh, that's great! I'm free at that time as well." She looked at me for confirmation.

I hesitated. This was an awkward position to be in. I needed more money to pay for school, but I wasn't thrilled that the word was spreading. Still, I nodded and said, "See you then." I was just about to move past her when a booming voice behind me caught me off guard.

"What's this I hear about readings?"

I whirled around.

Braydon Dudek stood directly behind me, a look of interest apparent on his round face.

"You scared me!" I had no idea he'd been behind us. How much had he heard?

He chuckled. "Sorry. Did I hear you say you were doing a reading? I'd love to participate. It's great actor training and a good way to test out a new play on an audience."

Cassandra wrinkled her nose. "A play?"

I nudged her with my elbow. "This isn't quite what you're thinking it is, Braydon. It's just a one-on-one reading."

"A one-person play?" His eyebrows arched.

Mila interrupted. "No, it's not a play. Jenny is giving me a psychic reading. I've heard she's really good."

Silence hung in the air.

"A psychic reading," he repeated in a flat tone, his expression unreadable.

"Yeah," Mila said. "I have a lot of questions I want answers to. Do you just do half-hour readings? Because I think an hour would be better for me."

"She can do an hour. But that costs fifty dollars instead of the twenty-five for the half-hour ones," Cassandra said.

April let out a low whistle and whispered to me, "Score. You're making some good money."

Cassandra elbowed her. "Does that work for you?"

Mila shrugged. "That's fine. I'll bring cash with me tomorrow morning."

Cassandra thanked her, and Mila continued down the hall.

We headed toward the vending machine with Braydon on my heels. "You're psychic?"

He was honestly the last person I wanted to know anything about me and what I could do. I stayed quiet.

"Well, are you?" He breathed down my neck.

Cassandra turned. "Of course she is. Haven't you been paying attention?" She stopped in front of the vending machine and took out a dollar. "Do I want a Snickers or a Twix?"

"Snickers has more protein," April offered helpfully.

"True." Cassandra fed the dollar into the slot and pushed the corresponding button for a Snickers bar.

April got herself a Snickers too, and then stepped aside so I could choose my treat.

I stood in front of the machine and saw Braydon's reflection in the glass. He was standing directly behind me—I could feel his stale breath ruffling my hair. I put my hand over my nose and mouth to keep from gagging. This guy was creeping me out.

I selected a big bag of strawberry fruit snacks. I watched as the machine whirred to life and the bag was pushed off its little ledge. It fell with a soft thud. The robotic mechanism swished it into the bottom tray. I reached in to retrieve it.

April and Cassandra had already begun their trek back to our room when Braydon grabbed my arm. "You fascinate me."

I was instantly repulsed by his touch. "Thanks?" I gently pulled my arm away and started to follow my friends.

He put his paw on my shoulder. "Would you like to go out sometime?"

Oh, God. There it was. I forced a smile. "Gee, Braydon, thank you for asking. But I have a boyfriend."

His expression was unreadable. "He doesn't have to know. I'm cool with sharing."

I stared at him. "Mike and I have a great relationship. I wouldn't even consider dating someone else and neither would he."

"Does he go to school here?" Braydon licked his lips.

"No. He goes to Ithaca."

"Then, he wouldn't know, and you don't have to tell him."

My jaw dropped. "Didn't you just hear what I said? I have no interest in dating someone else." This guy was so gross.

He shrugged. "All I ask is that you consider it. If you change your mind, let me know."

I would never change my mind. He wasn't ever going to get a date with me. I clenched my jaw and brushed by him, nearly sprinting to catch up to my friends.

When I looked back over my shoulder, he was still standing in the hall, staring at me.

Once we got back into our room, April asked, "What was that all about?"

I groaned. "He asked me out."

"Yuck." Cassandra ripped open her Snickers bar and took a bite. "You told him no, of course."

"Yeah. But he didn't like my answer. He said he was okay with sharing me with Mike." The thought sent a new wave of revulsion shooting through me.

"Double yuck." Cassandra took another bite. "Who does that?"

"Creepers?" April shrugged. "That guy is nasty. Did he even consider that you weren't into him? Stay as far away from him as you can."

"I've tried." I was exasperated. "But he's in my acting class. I can't completely avoid him." I opened my bag of fruit snacks. The scent of artificial strawberries filled the air. "Plus, it seems like everywhere I go—there he is."

"All you can do is put your walls up and to try and engage with him as little as possible." April pulled her half-dry hoodie off the end of Cassandra's bed. "I'm going to call campus security to see if they'll walk me back to my dorm."

"Want us to walk you?" Cassandra asked.

"No, no. There's no sense in all three of us getting soaked again. I'll be fine." She made the call and then opened the door. "They'll be down in just a few minutes. I'm going to wait in the lobby."

I changed into warm pajamas and stood by the window, watching to see that April made it safely across Washington

44

Square Park. Rain ran down the glass in streams. A bolt of lightning lit the sky and once again illuminated the tree where we'd seen the woman hanging.

The body flashed briefly into my field of vision, swaying from the thick branch she was hanging from.

Then she was gone.

# Chapter 7

My brain would not shut off and sleep seemed like an unattainable fantasy. My mind was determined to review every event, every person I'd told about my unique gift, and each obstacle I currently faced.

Staring up at the ceiling, I pulled the covers up to my chin and sighed. I turned my head to check the time again. The numbers on my bedside clock glared at me in neon red—three o'clock in the morning.

Maybe Mom was right. I shouldn't have gone to this school, no matter how great it was. She'd warned me about the expense, and I'd refused to listen. Somehow, I'd thought everything would magically work out, and I'd be able to afford tuition and all the extras. If she knew that I owed an additional two thousand dollars, she'd have a complete nervous breakdown. And a nervous breakdown was exactly where I was currently heading.

I rolled onto my side and tried to get comfortable.

But that didn't help either. I watched Cassandra sleep. She looked so peaceful and worry-free. She was curled up in a ball under her blankets, hugging her teddy bear. If only I could be like that.

My thoughts drifted to the reading I was doing for Mila tomorrow. I'd get fifty bucks that I could put toward the bill from the university. But, then what? How many readings would I have to do to get to two thousand dollars? Since I charged twenty-five dollars per half-hour session, that would be... eighty readings? Or, I could do forty one-hour readings. I'd have to give up sleep to do enough of them to meet the deadline. Would I have enough customers? Would I even *want* to do that?

There was only two and a half weeks left before the payment was due.

News of my special ability was already spreading. I thought about what would happen if I became known as that "psychic girl." Would my classmates treat me differently? Would directors use that as an excuse not to cast me?

I turned over on my other side. The light leaking in from the city through the window shade bored into my eyelids. I groaned and flung a pillow over my head.

After a long time of forcing myself to breathe, my body started to relax. My exhaustion finally led me into a deep sleep.

*The light turned red.*

*The best part of night in the city was now—when most people were sleeping.*

*I smiled and hummed to myself as I waited.*

*The trinity was almost complete. One more was all I needed.*

*The light turned green. I drove through the intersection and made a right. No one was behind me. I backed into the dark alley.*

*With my engine idling quietly and the headlights turned off, I got out of the van to wait.*

*I listened.*

*Footsteps echoed down the sidewalk. It was her.*

*I hurried to get back into the driver's seat and put the vehicle in drive. I kept my foot on the brake, savoring the moment before I rolled slowly out of the alley.*

*My heart pounded in anticipation. This was my favorite part. The resistance, the fear, and finally, the surrender.*

*The nose of the van eased onto the sidewalk.*

*There she was! Flawless in her scrubs and overcoat. She was more beautiful than I'd remembered. The perfect last piece to complete my destiny.*

*Her eyes shifted from her phone to my van. Fear creased her face.*

*The time was now.*

*I jumped out of the van and reached to grab her arm.*

*Her hand snatched something out of her coat pocket and before I could stop her, hot pain seared my eyes. A cloud of spray burned my skin.*

*She screamed and ran.*

*"Wait!" I coughed, tears flowing down my face, blurring my vision.*

*Anger exploded in my head. How dare she prolong my ecstasy?*

My eyes flew open. The alarm on my phone was chiming on the night stand next to my bed.

I sat up, my pulse ringing in my ears.

Cassandra popped up like a jack-in-the-box, her feet landing lightly on the floor. She stretched and grinned at me. "Good morning, sunshine!"

I let my head fall back on the pillow. "Ugh." Morning people shouldn't be so perky.

"You better get up. We should get breakfast before Mila arrives."

My head was pounding. "Can you hand me that bottle of ibuprofen on my desk?"

"Headache?"

"Yeah. I barely slept. I had another one of those weird dreams."

Cassandra handed me a bottle of water and two pills. "Here. Tell me about your vision."

After I told her everything I remembered, she said, "So, you were in this guy's head?"

I shrugged. "I guess you could say that. Not every vision or dream works the same way. Most of the time, I'm seeing through the eyes of the victim. In these recent dreams, though, I'm seeing through the eyes of this man. I can hear his thoughts. I see what he sees. I feel his emotions."

She bit her lip. "Jenny, the next time you have this dream, you've got to consciously try to see what he looks like."

"How would I do that?"

"Make him look in the rearview mirror or something. Or watch for his reflection in the window. You've got to pass this on to the police."

"I know, I know. I just don't have enough information to tell them yet. I didn't pay attention to the street signs. Maybe it's because he knew where he was, so his eyes didn't go there." I ran my fingers through my tangled hair. "I can barely give a description of the woman. She was maybe average height—slight build. Hard to identify her hair color. It was night, but I could tell the tone was a medium shade. It could've been brown or red. No other distinguishing attributes that I can think of."

Cassandra looked at the time. "Let's talk during breakfast. I'm starving."

I nodded. "Okay. But before I do Mila's reading, I'll do a meditation and try to see if I get anything more."

\*\*\*

After we returned from the cafeteria, I put the stones that Cassandra had given me in the center of my desk. I found a meditation playlist on Spotify, put in my earbuds, and played the music. I hoped it would help block out the noise of the city.

Cassandra packed up her laptop. "I'm going to go to a coffee shop to get some homework done. I'll see you in a couple of hours." Her voice was muted, but I was glad I could still hear her voice in spite of the music playing in my ears.

"Okay. Have fun." I smiled and closed my eyes.

"I will!"

Knowing Cassandra, she *would* have fun.

She shut the door behind her and left me to my thoughts.

I needed to learn more about the vision I'd had. There was a psycho out there, and I was certain he would try again. When I'd heard his thoughts in my head, one stood out in particular. *The trinity was almost complete. One more was all I needed.* It was absolutely chilling—he must already have abducted two women. Would that be enough information to go to the police with?

I sat with my hands, palms up, on my thighs. I took deep breaths, in through my nose, out through my mouth.

"God, spirit guides, and angels, please help me learn more about the man who is taking women. Help me discover his identity."

I visualized the white light of God surrounding me and connecting me to the energy of the universe. A feeling of love and safety enveloped me, and I knew the connection had been successful. From behind my eyelids, the daylight flooding my room dimmed. Darkness settled over me.

*I was back in his van at the time he tried to abduct the woman. It was as silent as it could get in a city that never sleeps. This time, I couldn't hear his thoughts. Instead of being inside his head, it was as if I was sitting on his shoulder—watching from his perspective, but not from within him.*

*His hands were on the steering wheel, but in the darkness, I couldn't pick out details. What color was his skin?*

*A street cleaner vehicle drove by, momentarily casting light into the driver's seat. White. His skin was fair.*

*What other things inside this van could help me identify who he was?*

*He was staring straight ahead. Waiting for his prey. Maybe when she entered his view, I could learn more about her, and find out who she was. I could warn her that he would try again.*

*There! She was walking with her head bent, scrolling on her phone. Her scrubs told me that she likely worked at a hospital or a 24-hour clinic of some sort.*

*She looked up.*

A knock on the door ripped me out of the vision. Damn.

I took a second to reorient myself. I was back in my room, sitting in my desk chair. The knock persisted.

Mila wasn't supposed to be here until eleven o'clock. I took out my earbuds and got up, already annoyed with the person on the other side of the door for ruining my chance to see the woman's face.

Braydon Dudek stood in the doorway. He was wearing a button-down shirt that didn't quite cover the bottom of his belly. His wrinkled chinos hung low on his waist. *Please, God*—I thought—*please don't let his pants fall down.*

"Hey, Jenny. I was just in the neighborhood and wondered if you'd like to hang out."

I blinked. "Uh, sorry, Braydon. Mila is coming over in just a few minutes."

"Right, right. I should've remembered. Maybe I could just sit on your bed while you do the reading? I won't make a sound. I promise."

I took a deep breath to keep myself from losing my temper. "That's not how it works. Readings are private. It's like visiting a therapist—you don't invite other people in to watch a counseling session."

"Oh. I see. How about I schedule a reading with you, then? For later, I mean."

"I'm pretty booked up for a while. Plus, I have a couple of monologues to memorize." I was proud of myself for keeping a steady, calm voice.

"Okay. I'll check back with you later. Because I'd love to have you do a reading for me. How much did you say they were?"

Crap. I was afraid he would suggest this. "They're twenty-five dollars per half hour, or fifty for one hour."

"Whoa! That's a lot of money. I bet you give discounts to *special* friends, right?" He gave me a smile that I could only interpret as him trying to be flirty.

"I'm sorry. I don't give discounts." His creepy vibes were starting to stress me out. Why did his energy feel so weird?

Mila peeked in through the open door. "We're still on for eleven, right?"

Relief rolled over me. "Yes! Come in." I gave her a big smile and turned to Braydon. "See you in class on Monday?"

He narrowed his eyes. "Yeah. Okay." He took a step back.

I closed the door gently and shook off his energy. Why wouldn't he just leave me alone?

"Make yourself comfortable." I pulled out a chair for Mila. "Would you like a bottle of water?"

# Chapter 8

It was Monday morning. We stood in the unadorned rehearsal room. The painted black walls and drab flooring were intended to keep us focused on our internal imagination. The same philosophy applied to what we were required to wear in acting class—black clothing, or "blacks," as we called them. Later, we would change into our leotards for ballet. Then, back into either blacks or street clothing for our voice classes.

Randy, our acting professor, began assigning scene partners. We were to speed-memorize our lines—then present our acts at the end of our two-hour class. I was getting better at memorizing, but I wasn't as fast as I wanted to be.

Randy called out the names for each set of partners. "Johnson and Carlie. Sam and Lexi, Braydon and Jenny."

Had I heard that right? Did he say—

"Well, well, well." Braydon suddenly stood before me. His once-white t-shirt was already pit-stained at eight-thirty in the morning. "So, we meet again," he said, in what he must've thought was a mysterious and sexy way.

I had the urge to throw up.

Randy finished reading through the list of scene partners. "Find a place away from others if you can, and work on your lines." He looked at his watch. "You've got an hour and fifteen minutes to work through your scenes together. For the last forty-five minutes, we'll watch everyone's presentations."

How could this be happening? Braydon was the last person I wanted to be teamed up with. There wasn't enough caffeine in the world to get me through this.

Braydon tugged on my arm and led me to the far corner of the room. He pulled me down to the floor with him. "Let's read through this a couple of times before we start memorizing."

Nice. Now he was my scene partner *and* my director.

Our scene was from the play, *Who's Afraid of Virginia Woolf?* I was assigned the part of Martha, and Braydon was playing George, her husband. I knew this play. I'd bought the script on my college visit in New York City before I was accepted to the university. The play was about a dysfunctional couple who were constantly arguing. They invite a younger married couple over for drinks and proceed to draw them into their awkward and drunken dysfunction.

Martha and George, though married, hated each other. I could easily play this part with Braydon. It wouldn't take much acting.

Braydon and I bantered back and forth as we rehearsed. I was surprised his acting was pretty decent. But, I didn't like that he was touching me more than I thought was necessary for the role. His fingers kept brushing my hair, and twice he put his hand at the small of my back.

"Okay, actors!" Randy called out. "Let's see what you've got." The tall, lanky man stood off to the side and called the first pair to the front.

My nerves kicked in as we watched the others perform their scenes, each from a different play. I scanned the script again, making sure I'd memorized my lines correctly.

"Braydon and Jenny." Randy pointed to us. "You're up."

We made our way to the front of the room.

I cleared my throat. "This is the opening scene of *Who's Afraid of Virginia Woolf*. I'm playing the role of Martha."

"And I'm playing the role of George," Braydon boomed.

I heard a few snickers from our classmates. I wondered if they'd also had some interesting encounters with him.

"Go ahead." Randy pushed his black-rimmed glasses up the bridge of his nose.

I took a deep breath and said the first line. "Jesus."

From there, the whirlwind of dialogue took me on a ride. I was Martha. Drunk and obnoxious—enjoying the sparring with her husband.

Braydon, too, seemed to be into the experience. I could see why he was accepted to our program. He was good. But that didn't mean that I liked him any more than I had than when class had begun.

When we finished our eight pages of dialogue, our classmates clapped and cheered.

Braydon and I took a bow.

"That was absolutely magical," Carlie said. She gave me a quick hug.

"Wasn't it though?" Braydon grinned broadly. "And speaking of magic, Jenny here has magic of her own. Right, Jenny?"

I froze. My stomach twisted.

Carlie gave him a curious glance.

"Everybody," he bellowed, "our very own Jenny Crumb is psychic. Just ask some of the students who've already had readings with her. I hear she's good."

Carlie's eyebrows shot up. She took a step backward.

I was sure my face reflected the same stunned look as my classmates'. A few beats of silence followed Braydon's announcement. I didn't know what to do. Everyone was clearly uncomfortable... and silent.

Randy seemed to come out of his stupor and stepped in to save me. "Uh, very funny, Braydon. Let's get on with class, shall we? Marcus and Will—you're up next."

For the rest of class, I couldn't hear the lines my peers were delivering. My hands clenched into fists, then relaxed. Clenched and relaxed. I couldn't wait to get out of the hot, stuffy rehearsal room. I needed to breathe—to run from the curious and shocked faces.

It was a mistake to come to this school. It was even a bigger mistake to let anyone know about my gift. How had I let this happen? If I'd only told Cassandra to keep it a secret, I wouldn't be going through this right now. That and the stupid bill for two thousand dollars. If it hadn't appeared in my pile of mail, I wouldn't have done that latest psychic reading—the one that Braydon had found out about.

Braydon. When I thought of him, my anger boiled over. Did he intentionally make me the laughingstock of our class? Or was he just *that* clueless?

Finally, the last pair of actors finished their scene. I slunk out of the room, trying not to make eye contact with anybody.

Braydon jostled his way over to me. I quickened my pace, nearly breaking into a full run to get away from him.

He was surprisingly fast and caught up to me. "Jenny— have you given more thought to my proposal?"

I gritted my teeth and kept walking at my brisk pace.

He caught up to me and touched my shoulder. "How about that date?"

I whirled. "Seriously? I told you no. I have a boyfriend. And even if I didn't, I wouldn't ever… ever… go out with you. After what you just did to me? I don't think I can even look at you again."

He regarded me for a moment. "That's too bad. It would be terrible if everyone found out about your little secret. Of course, I'm pretty good at keeping the secrets of the girls I date."

56

I reached out and clutched his arm.

*Flash.*
*My desk chair wasn't quite large enough for me to be comfortable.*
*The test scores mattered. Senior year mattered. Grades mattered.*
*I had to get into NYU. I had to prove to everyone that I was somebody.*
*This was the third test so far that I'd paid for. Two hundred dollars was a lot to shell out for the answers to the math final. But it had to be done. I was willing to pay if it meant I'd be someone my parents would be proud of.*

I breathed deeply. "I know your secret too, Braydon. Let's talk about the tests you cheated on to get into this school."

After watching Braydon make a hasty retreat, I walked to my voice lesson. Since he had basically outed me to my classmates, I just assumed I'd be treated like an outcast by the students who heard his announcement. What person in their right mind would want anything to do with me?

I blinked back tears. For some reason, I hoped I'd be regarded as just another first-year college student; awkward, naïve… maybe a little scared. Now, because of Braydon, I would have four years of being treated like a freak. A person to be avoided.

"Jenny?" A girl from my acting class tapped me on the shoulder.

I jumped.

"Sorry! I didn't mean to scare you." The girl smiled.

I quickly swiped at a tear that had begun its journey down my cheek. "That's okay, Cora."

"Listen," she said. "I'm sorry that Braydon did that to you. He's an idiot."

Her statement made me laugh, and suddenly I didn't feel as bad as I had just seconds ago. "He really is. Thank you for going out of your way to talk to me."

"No problem. Anyway, most of the people in our class have already had encounters with Braydon. He's pretty annoying. I wouldn't worry too much about what he said."

"I'm relieved to hear you say that." I felt lighter somehow. "I'm still trying to get to know people in our program. I thought Braydon would make it impossible for me to make friends."

"Not true." Cora swept her long dark hair off her shoulder. "People will side with you. They know he's a jerk."

I laughed. "Thank you."

She looked at the time on her phone. "Shoot. I've got to get to my next class, and it's quite a ways from here. See you in ballet?"

"Yup. See you in a few hours." I also had very little time to get to my voice lesson. But, I figured if I walked at a brisk pace, I'd make it there with no problem.

My phone buzzed. It was Mike. "Have a minute to talk?" he texted.

"Just a couple of minutes. On the way to my next class," I replied.

The phone buzzed again, this time with a call.

"Hi Mike."

"It's so good to hear your voice," he said. "I miss you."

"I miss you too." I sniffled a little.

"Are you okay?" Concern colored his voice.

I sighed. "I'm all right. Just a little overwhelmed. Lots of stuff going on."

"Like what? Is it just your schedule or is it something else?" he asked.

"Classes, learning my way around, and some personality issues too." I proceeded to tell him everything that had happened with Braydon so far. "So, I guess my emotions are getting the best of me right now."

"What an a-hole." Mike sounded angry. "When I come visit, I might just have to go have a talk with him."

"No, no. It's fine. I'll deal with him."

"Is there anything else bothering you besides that moron?"

I thought about my financial issues. I only had a couple of weeks to come up with two thousand dollars. "Just some money problems. But other than that, everything is fine. Ha ha." I explained about the unexpected bill I'd received. "And I can't tell my parents about it because they'd go ballistic. They're already upset that I chose to attend NYU. Tuition is so expensive."

Mike was silent for a few seconds. "I have a thousand dollars saved up from my summer job. How about I loan that to you? Then, you'll only have to come up with the remaining thousand."

I was shocked. "What? No! I can't do that."

"Why not?" he asked.

"Because I just can't. I'd feel really weird about that. I know something will come up. It has to."

"Okay," he said. "But if you change your mind, the offer will still be there."

"Thank you. I really appreciate it. But, I'll be fine." I glanced at the time. "I've got to get going. I don't want to be late for my voice lesson."

"I've got to go, too. Love you, Jenny. Talk to you soon?"

"Yes. For sure. Love you." I ended the call and walked into the small classroom to meet my vocal coach.

\*\*\*

After my lesson, I made my way to the cafeteria to grab an early lunch before getting ready for ballet class.

59

My phone buzzed again. I checked the screen. I had two missed calls from the same number that was calling me now. A number I didn't recognize. "Hello?"

A deep voice with a thick New York accent said, "Is this Jenny Crumb? This is Detective Jeff Caruso with the NYPD. My friend in Seattle gave me your name."

I stopped for a moment. "Oh, yes. Detective Coalfield told me that you might be contacting me."

"Great. He told me a little bit about your... expertise. I was wondering if you were available to meet at my precinct? I'd love to learn more about what you do."

"Oh. I guess so. Sure." My mind raced through my busy schedule. Maybe I shouldn't have told Detective Coalfield that it was okay for him to refer me. I still needed to find a job, and if helping the NYPD with something took a lot of time, I wouldn't be able to—

"Are you free this afternoon at around four o'clock?"

"I get out of class at three today," I said. "Where is your office?"

He gave me the address and told me which subway line to take. "Looking forward to meeting you, Jenny."

"You too." The call ended, and I stared at my phone. What was I doing? I didn't have time for this. My previous feelings of being overwhelmed returned. I squashed them down. I had to focus. Lunch—then ballet.

God help me.

# Chapter 9

At the precinct, I waited in a short line at the front desk. The woman behind it looked irritated—as if she'd just spoken to a crowd of annoying people.

When it was my turn, I gave her a meek smile. "I'm here to see Detective Caruso."

Her eyeroll and wry smirk made me feel like a little kid. "And your name is?"

"Jenny Crumb."

"Well, Jenny Crumb. Is he expecting you?"

I nodded. "Yes, he is."

My palms started to get sweaty. I rubbed them on my jeans. Why was I nervous? I almost felt like I'd done something wrong and was on my way to the principal's office.

A tall man with broad shoulders appeared at the end of the long hall. He had an olive complexion and dark, wavy hair which was graying at the temples. He cocked his head to one side. "Are you Jenny?"

"That's me."

He stuck out his hand, and I shook it. His grip was firm and dry. "Thanks for meeting with me. Come on back. I've reserved the conference room."

The drab room was large enough to accommodate a large table. There were at least twelve uncomfortable looking chairs situated around it. The walls were a nondescript gray. I wondered if the room was used for interrogations or meetings with the other detectives—or both.

"Have a seat," Detective Caruso said.

My nerves kicked in again. It felt weird being in this intimidating environment with a person I didn't know.

"So, Mark said some really great things about you."

I frowned. "Mark?"

He looked puzzled for a moment, and then laughed. "Mark Coalfield. I guess you wouldn't have known him by his first name."

"Oh." I felt foolish. "Detective Coalfield—of course!" My cheeks burned.

"He said you might be available to help us out. I have a few cases that I haven't made any headway on, and I think it would be good to see if your gift could help."

I hesitated. "Possibly. I don't know if he told you, but I'm a student at NYU, so my schedule is pretty busy."

He nodded. "Yes, he did mention that. We would appreciate any time you can give us."

"Okay." I shifted in my seat. "I'll do my best."

Detective Caruso cleared his throat. "Would you mind if I showed you some pictures? Just tell me if you have any impressions."

He opened up a folder he had in front of him and handed me the stack of photos.

Before I scanned any of them, I closed my eyes. I remembered the first time Detective Coalfield had shown me pictures of possible suspects in a kidnapping case. The photos of the men had completely unnerved me and left me sobbing. I'd seen every crime they'd committed—in graphic detail.

Celine, my mentor, had subsequently taught me to shield myself from the onslaught of those images and the feelings of fear that came with them.

With my eyes still closed, I imagined a white light surrounding me. I silently asked God, the angels, and my spirit guides to let me see the information I needed to see. I asked for their protection and to shield me from the fear that the victims may have felt.

When I was finished, I opened my eyes and looked at the top photo. It was a mugshot of a man with short dark hair.

*Flash.*

*The man was sitting at a desk in an office.*

*A framed picture was perched on the corner of his desk. In the photo, a pretty woman and three small children smiled as they played in a swimming pool.*

*The office was full of activity. A police woman walked in and led a man to a chair in front of her desk. "Have a seat, Mr. Dixon." She sat behind her computer. "Can you tell me exactly what was stolen from your apartment?"*

*The man who had the photo on his desk stood up and put on his jacket. The silver badge he picked up glinted under the fluorescent lights.*

*The police woman looked up. "Are you taking off, Manuel?"*

*"Yep. It's the wife's birthday. I've got to pick up some flowers and a cake."*

*She grinned. "She's trained you well."*

*The man laughed. "Don't I know it."*

I opened my eyes. "He's not a suspect. He's a cop. His name is Manuel. He has a wife and three kids."

Detective Caruso's eyebrows arched. "Well, I'll be darned."

I was irritated. Why was he wasting my time on something like this? Was he just testing me? I opened my mouth to say something but changed my mind. Maybe playing along with his little game would be best for now. At least until I could figure out what he wanted from me.

I flipped the photo over and looked at the next one. It was of a young woman with shoulder-length light brown hair. Was it a senior photo? She looked to be about eighteen years old.

Placing my hand on the photo, I again closed my eyes.

*Flash.*

*The beach grass fluttered in the summer wind, and the brine of the ocean filled my nostrils.*

*The girl from the photo ran barefoot on the sand, her hair flowing behind her. She was wearing a soft, flowy dress sprinkled with a flower print.*

*A man stood on the ridge, far back from the water. He watched the girl with intensity.*

*The girl turned around and shouted, "Brian! Hurry up! We're late to the party!"*

*I felt my body rise up in the air—so that I had a bird's eye view of the beach. The sun was slowly setting on the horizon, coloring the water with an orange sherbet brush. A bonfire was blazing further up the beach, and several dozen teens were gathered around it, sitting on logs or throwing more driftwood into the fire.*

*I saw the girl running, and behind her, at least one hundred yards back, was a boy—presumably Brian. He was carrying an armful of firewood.*

*The man who watched the girl run, turned to look at Brian.*

*I swooshed from the sky and into the man's body. Now I was seeing through his watchful eyes. I didn't hesitate. When Brian stumbled, dropping his armload of firewood, I darted out onto the beach and grabbed the girl.*

*She tried to scream, but I had her in a choke hold. I dragged her away from the sand and into the brush. She struggled like a wildcat. I couldn't let her call attention to us.*

*"Chelsea?" Brian called. "Where did you go?"*

*With my hand over her mouth, she still tried to scream, but only mewling sounds were escaping. I had to keep her quiet. I wrapped my hand around her throat and squeezed. There. That was better. She didn't make a sound. She didn't even move.*

My eyes opened wide, and a gasping sound escaped my throat. My hands rubbed my neck.

"Jenny? Are you okay?" Detective Caruso leaned forward in his chair.

I took a deep breath in and exhaled slowly. "I'm okay. But this girl isn't. She's dead."

The detective nodded. "We found her body a week ago."

"Then, why did you show me this picture of her?" I couldn't hide the irritation.

He looked mildly apologetic. "Sorry. I had to see if what Detective Coalfield said about you was true. I had to see it for myself."

I was still slightly annoyed. "Okay. I get that." I took a breath and made myself relax. "Her name was Chelsea. She died somewhere on the coast. She was headed for a bonfire with her friends. There was a boy named Brian—he was behind her. But he didn't see the man who took her."

"Do you know who killed her?" he asked.

"No. I didn't see his face. But if you'd like, I can work on getting some details about him."

"I would like that very much. Let me know if you need anything. Maybe an article of clothing from the victim?"

"I don't know if clothing would help. But—I would like to see the area where she was killed. Is it close by?"

65

"Sort of. It's Rockaway Beach. Her family owns a vacation home in the area. It's an hour drive from here."

"Okay. I don't have a car. Should I take a train or something like that?"

"If you're free this weekend, I can drive you. Besides, we don't have anyone in custody. It's not safe for you to be there alone without police protection."

"That would be good." I didn't like the idea of traveling there on my own.

His eyes drifted to the remaining photo in front of me. "Care to try one more?"

"Sure." I was getting tired, but if I could help someone who wouldn't otherwise be found, I would try.

The next photo was of a small boy. He looked to be about five or six years old. He had light brown hair, big brown eyes, and a gap-toothed smile. My heart sank. Oh, God. I hated it when bad things happened to little kids.

I closed my eyes and placed my hand on his picture.

*Flash.*

*The new nanny, Gia, was acting funny.*

*She usually took me to Central Park after school.*

*Today, she took me in a different direction.*

*"Aren't we going to the park?"*

*She shook her head. "Not today. Today is special. How about ice cream?"*

*I nodded. I loved ice cream!*

*We walked a long way.*

*"Where is the ice cream shop?" I looked up at her.*

*She looked worried. That made me feel scared.*

*A tall lady waited at the corner. Her face looked hard, like a statue. She nodded at Gia and reached her hand out to me. "Come. We need to hurry," she said.*

*I frowned. "Who is that lady, Gia?"*

*Gia let go of my hand. "Her name is Diane. She will take you to get ice cream."*

*I stepped backward. "But I don't know her. I'm not supposed to go with strangers."*

*Gia gave me a weird smile. "She's not a stranger. She's nice. Go with her."*

*My eyes darted back to the stranger. She didn't look friendly. She scared me.*

*"No!" I turned and ran. I had to get away.*

*I looked behind me. Gia and the scary lady were chasing me!*

*I ran, and ran, and ran. At the next corner, I saw the subway sign. I went down the stairs as fast as I could. In my pocket was the metro card Mama gave me for emergencies. I was pretty sure this counted as an emergency, so I ran the card through the slot. The E train was coming. The noise almost drowned out the yelling from the top of the stairs.*

*Gia yelled, "Andrew!"*

*The doors opened.*

*I got on.*

*I watched her run down the stairs. She was coming!*

*The doors closed.*

*Her angry face disappeared as the train went faster down the track.*

I opened my eyes.

"The little boy's name is Andrew, right?"

Detective Caruso nodded, wide-eyed. "His mother reported him missing this morning. She'd left him with the nanny while she went shopping."

I bit my lip. "The nanny, Gia, tried to give him to a tall woman named Diane."

The detective leaned forward in his chair.

"But Andrew knew he shouldn't go with strangers. He sensed something was very wrong."

"Did this Diane take him?" he asked.

"No." I took a deep breath and let it out. My heart was still hammering in my chest. "Andrew ran. He took the E

67

train somewhere. Gia ran after him, but she was too late. Thank God."

"Do you know what direction he went? Or what the street names were?"

I shook my head. "No. I only know what I told you."

"This is great information. Hang on." He got up and left the room.

It seemed like a long time had gone by, and there was no sign of Detective Caruso. I was about to go find out what was going on. Just as I got up, he came back into the room, carrying a soda, a bag of chips, and a sheet of paper.

He slid the soda and chips toward me. "Thought you might be hungry."

"Thanks. I am." I opened the bag of chips and popped the soda can open.

"Sorry that took so long. We sent out officers to every stop the E train runs along. They just now found Andrew wandering near Roosevelt Avenue, thanks to you."

I sat up straighter. "Is he all right?"

He nodded. "He's fine. Scared. But fine."

"What do you think happened? Why was the nanny handing him off to a stranger?"

He shrugged. "We're investigating. It could be that it was a ransom thing. We don't know yet."

He slid a sheet of paper toward me.

"What's this?" I stared down at the paper.

Detective Caruso reached out for a handshake. "It's a job offer. Welcome to the NYPD, Jenny."

# Chapter 10

On the subway ride back to my dorm, I felt lighter. Detective Caruso had offered me a consultant position. I had no idea how much it paid, but the fact of the matter was—I had a job.

When I got back to my room, Cassandra was sitting at her desk with her laptop open. Her fingers flew over the keys with the speed of a cheetah. The sound of the door closing behind me made her pause. "Oh, hey." She continued typing.

"What are you working on?" I put my purse down.

"I'm writing a paper on how Florentine art depicts women of all shapes and sizes, as a comparison of how modern media views women's bodies today." She continued to type even as she spoke.

"Wow. Sounds cool." I noticed a few pieces of mail on my desk. "Thanks for picking up the mail."

"No problem." The keys kept up the frenetic clickety-clacking sound.

The top envelope was from the university. It said, "Important."

I groaned. The bill wasn't due for two weeks. Already, they were sending intimidating letters.

I tore open the envelope. The two-thousand-dollar amount was highlighted in yellow. I checked the time It was after five o'clock. The office was probably closed. I would call them in the morning to see if I could work out a payment plan. I thought about my new job and wondered how often they paid. Once a month? Every other week? I wished I'd asked Detective Caruso those questions. But I was so stunned that I'd gotten a job, I hadn't thought to ask.

"You got another statement from NYU." Cassandra kept typing.

"I know. I'll work something out with them after I get my first paycheck."

The typing stopped abruptly. "You got a job?"

"I did." I couldn't hold back the grin that was plastered on my face.

"Woohoo!" Cassandra flung herself at me and gave me a rib-crushing hug.

I laughed and pulled myself away to breathe. "Thanks."

"So, should I stop telling people about your psychic readings?" Cassandra situated herself at her laptop again.

I thought for a moment, feeling the sting of Braydon's proclamation in class and how everyone had stared. "Well, I don't know how much the NYPD will pay me. But let's hold off until I know if I need to make more money or not."

She nodded. "Okay." Her fingers resumed their supersonic dance across the keyboard.

Slipping off my shoes, I grabbed my laptop and climbed onto my bed. Now was the time to get some homework done. I pulled up the PDF of the monologue I had to memorize for acting class.

My phone buzzed. It was a text from my best friend, Benny. He'd just started his senior year at Newport High School back home.

"Hey!"

I texted. "What's up?"

"I'm visiting colleges with Frank in a couple of weeks. We're stopping in NYC."

"Yay!" I replied. "Are you coming to see Cassandra and me?"

"Duh. How could I not?" he texted.

I looked up from my phone. "Cassandra—Benny and Frank are visiting us soon." I said.

"What? That's great!" Cassandra said. "I can't wait to see them."

I relayed the message to Benny, then asked, "Which schools are you visiting out here?"

"Columbia, NYU, Pace, Marymount Manhattan College, and Ithaca."

"Awesome. Let's meet up." I hit send.

"Yup. Text you when I know more," he said.

Cassandra stood by our wireless printer and watched her essay print out. "You know, I wish Duncan could visit sooner than Thanksgiving break. I miss him so much."

"Maybe I can convince Mike to come down for an early visit too."

Duncan was Cassandra's boyfriend. We'd met him on our summer vacation in Europe. He was a handsome Scottish guy—the nephew of Professor Greenbough. The professor and Duncan had just started doing research of the Salem witch trials. He and Duncan were doing an assessment of the witch hunt in Europe in parallel with the witch hunt in the United States.

Cassandra's eyes misted over. "I'm dying to see him again."

I gave her a rueful smile. "Long distance relationships are hard."

"Yeah." She picked up the pages as they came out of the printer. "The only way to get through it is to concentrate on school."

"Good point." I turned my attention back to my homework.

71

A few hours later, we were done with our work, in our pajamas, and tucked into bed, the lights of the city muted by our window shade.

"Good night, Jenny." Cassandra rolled over and faced the wall.

"Good night." I closed my eyes and fell asleep almost immediately.

*Her shift was ending.*
*I waited outside, knowing which route she'd be taking.*
*The minutes went by too slowly.*
*Where was she?*
*My patience eroded with time.*
*How dare she keep me waiting?*
*Finally, I walked back to my van.*
*I would try again tomorrow. The others were expecting me.*

I sat straight up in bed, panic rising in my chest. The man I'd dreamed of was still chasing the woman who wore scrubs. Which hospital had he been waiting in front of? Even though I didn't have any useful information for the police, I knew I had to tell them. If I didn't, I was sure the woman would be abducted.

My fingers reached for the phone on the desk next to my bed. I checked the time. It was three o'clock in the morning.

I couldn't call the detective at this hour. This wasn't an emergency. Yet.

Sliding back down under the covers, I settled on my back and stared at the ceiling until sleep finally came.

When the alarm went off, my eyes were heavy with sleep. How could it be morning already? It didn't seem possible.

A few minutes later, the snooze alarm went off again. I opened my eyes to see Cassandra standing in front of my bed, her arms crossed.

"It's about time, sleepyhead. We're going to be late for breakfast." She peered at my face, her annoyance changing to concern. "God. You look awful. Rough night?"

I yawned. "Yeah. Bad dreams."

"The same one as last time? With the scary man?" She sat down at the foot of the bed.

"Same man. But this time, he was waiting for the woman in front of the hospital where she works. Luckily, he didn't get her."

"So, she's a doctor?" Cassandra asked.

I shrugged. "I don't know. She's some kind of medical person. She wears scrubs. That could be a doctor, a nurse, or an orderly."

"You should tell the police." She stood up.

"No one has gone missing yet, so I don't know if it will help. But I'm going to call the detective right now. Then, we'll go get something to eat." I picked up my phone and called him.

"Detective Caruso," he said.

"It's Jenny Crumb, Detective. I have a weird question."

"What is it?"

"I should've told you this before, but I've been having a few scary premonitions. Have there been any reports of missing women? Two, to be exact?" I held my breath.

There was a pause. "There are people going missing every day. That's not unusual though. Any particular descriptions besides that they're women?"

"Let me try to put it in context," I said. "I've been having dreams of a man who is stalking women. The first woman was a jogger. He got her by hiding behind a dumpster. When she ran by, he grabbed her."

The detective was quiet.

73

I continued. "The second one was dressed in business casual, probably on her way to work. She went into a coffee shop, and when she came out, he was waiting for her. He drives a white van. He parked it in the loading zone outside the coffee shop."

"Hmm. What does the man look like?" he asked.

"I don't know. All I know is that he's white."

"Well, that's better than nothing. Got anything else?"

I sighed. "I'm sorry. I wish I had more information."

"How about the women?" he asked. "What did they look like?"

"The first woman, the jogger, had long hair. She wore it in a ponytail. The man grabbed her by the hair when he snatched her off the sidewalk."

"Old? Young? Did you see her face or see any other identifying features?"

"Young. Maybe mid-twenties or early thirties. But again, I can't tell you what either woman looked like. It happened too fast."

"Anything else?" he asked.

"He's after another woman. He's stalking her, but he hasn't been able to catch her yet."

I described the two dreams I'd had with the woman in scrubs.

"Any idea which hospital? Did you see a sign or any landmarks in the area? New York City has over sixty-two hospitals in our five boroughs."

Frustration rose inside me. If I'd only paid more attention to surroundings when I was seeing through the eyes of the kidnapper. "I'm sorry. I just don't know the city well enough to know where the man was. Or where the women were taken from."

"That's all right. I'll check to see if there are any new reports on missing women that match your account. In the meantime, if you have any more dreams or visions about them, let me know right away. Sound good?"

74

"Yes." I felt a little better after telling him about the women. I hoped they were still alive, and that we could find and warn the woman he was stalking. "Thank you."

\*\*\*

We met up with April at the cafeteria downstairs.

Cassandra closed her eyes and munched on a piece of bacon. "Mmm. It doesn't get any better than this."

April wrinkled her nose. "Yuck. You're eating a cute little animal."

Cassandra stopped, mid-munch and said in her sternest voice. "Do not ruin this for me."

I laughed. Cassandra had worshiped bacon since I'd first met her in Sitka.

"Are you a vegetarian, April?" I took a sip of tea.

She nodded. "For about ten years now. I'm an animal lover. I just can't eat meat in good conscience. But I do eat eggs and dairy."

Cassandra looked sullen while she ate her food.

April noticed her friend's gloomy demeanor. "Hey, I'm sorry. I shouldn't have said anything. Just because I don't eat meat doesn't mean that you can't."

Cassandra shrugged and peeled a banana. She still looked upset, but I could tell her sullenness was wearing off. She couldn't stay upset about anything for more than five minutes.

Changing the subject seemed like a good idea. "Did Cassandra tell you I got a job?"

"No, she didn't. Congratulations!" April grinned.

We talked at length about my dreams, Detective Caruso, and the weird things that happened when he showed me the photos.

"Well, now you're turning me into a believer," she said. "Did you say you're going to the site where that girl was killed on the beach?"

75

"This weekend. Detective Caruso is going to drive me there."

"Wow. That is so cool. I wonder if you can help find the killer?" Her eyes had grown bigger. "That would be awesome."

"I hope so. I don't want anyone else to get killed if that guy is still walking around free." I finished my toast and wiped my hands on a napkin.

"Would Detective Caruso mind if we came along?" Cassandra stood and picked up her tray.

I shrugged. "I don't know. But I'd feel kind of funny taking friends with me. It doesn't seem very professional."

"I get it. But if April and I can help you in any way, let us know." She dumped her garbage and set the tray in the rack. "I need to get to class early. We're doing figure drawing this morning, and I want to pick my spot to draw before everyone else gets there."

"You want to get a seat in front of the nude model, huh?" I teased.

She snorted. "No. Gross. I could do without the crotch shot, thank you very much."

April let out a guffaw. "You West Coast people are pretty prudish."

"Right." Cassandra lightly punched April's arm. "Not as prudish as you Southern girls."

# Chapter 11

On Saturday morning, I got up early and grabbed a coffee and a pastry to take with me on the subway. Just as I was about to open the door, a big hand reached for the handle. I turned to see who'd blocked my way out.

It was Braydon Dudek.

"Well, well. If it isn't Jenny Crumb."

That seemed to be his favorite phrase of late. I clenched my jaw. "Hello, Braydon."

"Where are you off to so bright and early on a Saturday morning?"

"Just off to run some errands."

"Care if I tag along? I've got nothing planned today."

Ugh.. This guy was something else. "I do care, actually. I have some things I need to do on my own."

"Like what?"

I stepped past him and opened the door. "Like—that's my business."

He followed me out the door. "You don't have to be so snippy. I understand that some women like to play the cat and mouse game with men—but you don't have to do that with me. I've already told you, I'm interested."

I narrowed my eyes. "You might be interested, Braydon. But I'm not."

He stood silent as I stormed out.

When I turned to look behind me, he was gone.

*\*\**

I met Detective Caruso at the precinct. He pointed to the vehicle parked in a space marked "police only."

We got into the car. I put my day bag between my feet and sipped the rest of my coffee. "Thanks for driving me over to Rockaway Beach. I would've had a tough time getting there myself."

"Don't mention it. I wouldn't feel right about you going alone. The police in that jurisdiction still haven't caught the killer. The entire neighborhood is terrified. That's why they've asked us our precinct for help." He started the engine and expertly navigated the vehicle through the crowded city streets.

"Can you tell me more about how your gift works?" He turned on the blinker and made a right at the intersection.

I thought for a moment before answering. "You know, that's a really good question. I'm not sure how it works. Sometimes, I have dreams and sometimes I have what I call 'flashes.' But it's never completely predictable. I never know how or what I'll pick up on."

"Interesting. Your gift would be especially useful in my job. Have you considered a career in criminal justice or law enforcement? The FBI would also be a good match for you. You could be a profiler."

"I guess I've never given it much thought. I'm a musical theatre major."

"Really? Wow, I couldn't have been further off track, huh?" He laughed.

I smiled. "Well, who knows? I could be the world's first stage actress detective."

"There is a lot of drama in every police department. It might be a good fit." His grin spread, and he chuckled.

"My dad would argue that you don't know real drama until you've had a teenage daughter." I grinned.

By the time we reached Rockaway Beach, we were comfortable with one another. I learned all about his wife, Lynn, and their two young kids, and he learned about me and my life back home in the Pacific Northwest.

We pulled into a parking lot at one end of the beach. The lot was mostly full, except for a few random spots.

I got out of the car, careful not to let the door bang against the Mercedes next to us.

The wind whipped at my hair, sending it flying around my face. The briny smell of the water reminded me of home. Sort of. The air was missing the scent of cedar and fir trees. But, it was still exhilarating to feel the wild nature of the ocean.

"This way." Detective Caruso pointed down to the more remote end of the beach.

The opposite end of the shoreline was tourist-friendly and prettier to look at. This end, however, was bare and industrial-looking.

There were scrubby bushes and a few outbuildings here and there. We walked down a little road to the beach. The shore was so long, I couldn't tell where the beach started and where it ended.

Detective Caruso pointed toward a spot were a run-down shed stood. There was a small hill, covered with beachy vegetation. "Chelsea was found over here."

I walked to the place and stood with my feet planted in the sand.

Closing my eyes, I silently asked Chelsea to come forward and show me the man. With my eyes closed, I waited until I felt the familiar nudge of energy from a spirit. She was here. Her energy was beautiful, and I felt she was at peace. I told her that I was glad she was happy. But I needed to see the killer who'd taken her life. I needed enough information so the police could arrest him—so he couldn't take the life of any other person.

She agreed to help. While my body stood next to the detective, my spirit left with Chelsea. This was extraordinary, and the first time anything like this had happened to me. Maybe it was because she had her own talents, which she'd extended to me while in my presence. But the time to wonder was later. Now, we needed to find the man.

We flew away from the water, up several side streets until we reached an older apartment building on James Street. It was a fairly small structure, with only eight units. She led me to the lobby and showed me the buttons next to each resident's name. Guests would push the button of the person they'd come to visit, and then the resident could buzz them in.

She pointed to the name on apartment number five. Marsden O'Donnell. I nodded and let her know I understood.

Chelsea touched my arm, and suddenly, we were standing in his studio apartment. It was filthy. Dirty dishes were piled high in the sink. A cockroach made its purposeful march toward a clump of something brown on the countertop.

She pointed toward Marsden O'Donnell. He was seated at his computer, scrolling through what looked like porn pages. Violent scenes of young women being hurt. The photos there would've turned my stomach, had my spirit been in my human body.

I looked away. Chelsea nodded. It was time to go. We flew back down the streets, until my spirit slid back into my body still standing on the beach.

My legs gave out underneath me, and I fell to the sand.

"Are you all right?" Detective Caruso asked.

I took in a few deep breaths and tried to orient myself.

"I'm all right. His name is Marsden O'Donnell. He lives close by, on James Street, apartment number five. He's home right now."

\*\*\*

I waited for what seemed like forever in the detective's car while he got a warrant to search O'Donnell's apartment. Since I had some time on my hands, I reached into my bag for my laptop. Homework was due tomorrow. Surprisingly, I was able to concentrate while the action played out down the street.

By the time the detective returned, I'd gotten all of my work done and was about to start reading ahead in my acting class textbook when he returned.

"Sorry about the wait." He got in and closed the door. "I got the warrant pretty quickly, and we made the arrest. We can head back to the city now." He turned to look at me. "What you did back there was amazing. Thank you."

"You're welcome." I suspected that he had confidence in me. Now was the time to ask him about the missing women.

"Detective, remember how I told you about the dreams I've been having about a man who's abducting women?"

He nodded. "I remember."

"Is there any way to check and see if those women I described are missing? As a new consultant for the NYPD, am I allowed to look through your system for missing persons? I might recognize them—even if the glimpse of them in my dreams was vague."

"I think I can arrange that. But not today. I've got a mountain of paperwork to complete on the O'Donnell case. Come by next week sometime, and I'll see what I can do. Call beforehand, though."

"I will."

We arrived at the NYU campus, and he pulled into a loading zone to let me out.

As I was getting out of the car, he said, "Good work today."

"Thanks."

I watched his car drive away. It turned left at the next light and was gone.

Wow. That experience was a mix of adrenaline high and utter and complete exhaustion. It seemed surreal. I'd helped catch a killer. The feeling I'd done something good by helping take a killer off the streets was exhilarating. I wanted to do more of that.

I turned to walk to my dorm and slammed right into Braydon Dudek's soft chest. "Braydon! What are you doing here?"

"The better question is, what are you doing getting out of an unmarked police car?" He looked down at me, his face expressionless. "I can tell those things from a mile away—those large side mirrors and dark tinted windows—dead giveaway."

"I don't need to answer that." I tried to walk past him.

He put his hand on my shoulder. "Are you in trouble with the law?"

"No!" My tone was indignant. "Of course not. And why are you stalking me? It seems like everywhere I go, there you are."

Braydon raised his eyebrows. "I was just going about my business and happened to see you get out of that car." He pointed in the direction Detective Caruso had turned. "Are you having an affair with a cop? I mean, why would you choose that old guy when you could have me?"

"Seriously?" My voice had an edge to it. I didn't often lose my temper, but when I did, it wasn't pretty. "Who do you think you are, accusing me of sleeping with a police officer?"

He held his hands up in the air, as if he were surrendering. "Hey, calm down. When I see something odd, I call it like it is. I believe in transparency. You told me you had a boyfriend. In fact, you told me that's why you didn't want to go out with me. And here I see you fraternizing with law enforcement. That's a double standard, Jenny. I'm disappointed in you."

"For your information, I'm not sleeping with a cop. And even if I was, which I'm not, it would be none of your business."

"So, why were you with him then?"

I was done. "I'm not having this conversation with you." I shouldered past him and stormed off to my dorm.

***

Later, in my room, I was having a video call with Mike.

My heart melted when I saw his handsome face. His green eyes sparkled, along with his genuine smile.

"Hey, babe. It's so good to see you," he said.

"I really miss you." I wanted to reach out and touch him through the screen.

"I miss you too. But, I hope to visit next weekend. Is that okay?"

The anger which still lingered over the encounter with Braydon disappeared in an instant. Joy surged through me, and I clapped my hands with excitement. "Next weekend? I thought you were coming in two weeks."

Mike laughed. "I had to switch some things around a bit. I just found out I got cast as Sweeney Todd in our class's fall production. Rehearsals start on the following Monday."

"Congratulations! I'm so proud of you. Whatever the reason for being here sooner, I'm so happy you're visiting."

We spent the next hour talking about theatre, our classes, and how different life was from our home in the

Pacific Northwest. I told him about Braydon and how it seemed like he was following me.

"When I come down there, let me deal with him. For now, try to avoid him."

"I've already tried avoiding him. He just keeps shadowing me. And I have acting class with him, so there's not much I can do about that."

"Do your best, and if you feel threatened at any point, call campus police." His concern for me warmed my heart.

"That's a good plan. Text me when you leave Ithaca on Friday."

"I will. My bus leaves at four o'clock in the afternoon. I should be there by eleven, at the latest."

"Okay. I'll get you a guest pass and meet you in the lobby when you get here."

# Chapter 12

It was Monday, and the two-thousand dollar payment was due at the financial aid office next week. I hadn't yet gotten my paycheck from the NYPD, but I did have fifty dollars from my previous readings that I could put toward the balance. This morning, I'd called and arranged to make partial payments. I just hoped that fifty dollars would be enough to show them I intended to pay it off eventually.

"I'll go with you." Cassandra put on her shoes and slung her backpack onto one shoulder.

"Don't you have to get to class?" I opened the door and we headed for the stairs.

"Class was canceled because the professor is sick. I was just going to get some coffee and study anyway. Hanging out with you sounds like more fun."

"Standing in line at the financial aid office won't be very exciting. Are you sure?"

"Of course!" She bounded down the stairs, her backpack bouncing up and down as she went.

The cafeteria was busy, but we managed to each get a cup of coffee quickly.

"Hey, guys." April stood with a travel mug in hand.

"April!" Cassandra nearly knocked the cup out of her friend's hand as she hugged her. "Happy Monday."

April rolled her eyes. "Yeah, whatever. I haven't had enough caffeine yet for it to be happy."

"We're going to the financial aid office." Cassandra opened the door for April. "Want to come?"

"I've got to get to class. But I'm headed that way. I'll walk with you."

The day was muggy and overcast, and it looked like it might rain later in the day.

Students were making their way across the square, in an unorganized fashion. Some were on the sidewalks, walking briskly. Others didn't seem to be in a hurry. They meandered diagonally through the grass, looking at their phones or chatting with friends.

We took a shortcut through Washington Square Park even though the grass was wet with dew. Once we walked past the arch, goosebumps prickled my arms and neck, and I shivered.

There was something about this place that seemed off. Something creepy.

"Are you all right?" April raised one eyebrow. "You look a little dazed."

Dazed was a good word. I felt dazed and maybe even a little dizzy.

I blinked and the world changed.

*Flash.*
*The sound of shovels scraping dirt made my skin crawl.*
*Thunk.*
*Scrape.*
*Thunk.*
*Scrape.*
*The grass at my feet turned to dirt.*
*It piled around my ankles.*
*Then my knees.*
*Thunk.*
*Scrape.*

*Panic welled up inside me.*
*All around me, there were bodies.*
*Thunk.*
*Scrape.*
*The dirt reached my mouth.*
*I tilted my chin up and gasped for air.*
*Thunk.*
*Scrape.*
*When the dirt rose up into my nostrils, everything went black.*

"Jenny?" Cassandra was kneeling beside me on the grass. "What happened?"

Gasping for air, I looked around. I felt foolish, sitting on the grass, where I must've sunk to my knees. I prayed that no one had seen me go down.

"I'm fine." I got up and brushed bits of grass from my jeans. They were wet where my body had met the grass. "Great. It looks like I peed on myself."

April laughed. "No, it doesn't. Not unless it ran down your butt and the outside of your thigh."

Cassandra touched my arm. "What happened?"

I explained the vision I'd had.

April winced. "That's super weird and scary. I'm glad I don't have what you have."

Cassandra shrugged. "I think it would be cool. I've always admired your gift. I wish I had even a little bit of your ability."

"Careful what you wish for," I said. "It's not all fun and games. But you've been around me long enough to know that."

She grinned. "Yeah. But I still think it's cool. Come on." She grabbed my hand. "Let's go see about your payments."

April had veered off the path. "I'll catch up with you later for dinner."

87

When we got to the financial aid office, there was already a line.

"So, what do you think your vision is about?" Cassandra set her backpack down at her feet as we stood waiting.

"I have no idea. I had a similar creepy feeling walking through there last week."

"And don't forget that woman hanging from the tree during the thunderstorm." Cassandra pushed her pack forward with her foot as we scooted toward the front of the line.

"The worst part is not knowing how all these things fit together." I took another step forward. "Or if they fit together at all."

"Yeah." Cassandra frowned. "I guess we need to wait and see if you have another vision that offers more information."

We reached the front, and a woman behind a sliding glass window waved us over. "What can I help you with?" she asked.

I put the bill for $2,000 on the desk. "Hi. I received this statement and I was wondering if I could make partial payments without getting a late fee?"

She adjusted her reading glasses. "Oh, this one. I wish the university would just roll this into tuition. But yes, we can do partial payments."

"Oh, good. I'm relieved!" I took out the fifty dollars from my pocket. "I just got a part-time job, but I won't get my paycheck for a while. Will this do as a small payment for now?"

She gave me a look filled with empathy. "Of course, dear. I know how expensive college is these days. When I went to school, tuition was only six thousand dollars a year. Can you imagine that?"

I shook my head. "No. I can't. I wish it still was."

She smiled. "Students have to work a lot harder at everything in today's world. I'll mark this as a partial payment and will look forward to you bringing what you can in the next few months."

"Thank you!"

"That was nice," Cassandra said. "I was expecting her to be mean, like the people at the DMV."

I grinned, feeling better. "Me too."

As we headed to our separate classes, Cassandra waved. "See you this afternoon."

Waving goodbye, I turned toward the theatre building.

I glanced back toward the big white arch in the park. I dreaded walking back across Washington Square Park alone this afternoon.

# Chapter 13

I was about to walk out of the last class of the day, when one of my professors stopped me. "Jenny, are you able to stay for a bit? I'm writing a play and it's nearly finished. But, I'm having trouble with one scene. It's between two unlikely lovers who are in the midst of deciding whether or not to continue their relationship."

Feeling flattered that she would ask me to participate, I agreed.

"Follow me." She led me down the hall to one of the rehearsal rooms.

When she opened the door, I stopped walking in mid-stride. Braydon Dudek was sitting on the floor, cross-legged, reading the script.

Why was the universe constantly putting me in the path of this jerk?

My mentor, Celine, had once told me that we are presented with lessons here on earth. When we're first offered a life lesson, the universe gently taps us on the shoulder if we don't learn from it right away. If we ignore the message we're supposed to learn, the universe gets a bit louder. It throws another obstacle of the same nature in our path. And if we still don't learn from that, the universe makes the next attempt bigger, louder, and nastier. It was best to learn the lesson right from the beginning, if at all possible.

What was I supposed to learn from my encounters with Braydon? Should I be more forgiving of someone who didn't have the capacity to take no for an answer? Should I be more forceful in letting him know I wanted nothing to do with him? Maybe I was supposed to sidestep him while I kept on my own path. I had no idea.

My only choice was to pick one strategy and go with it. If it didn't work, I'd try the next tactic.

I decided that today, I would be kind to him. But I'd avoid any talk about dates or relationships.

Braydon looked up from his script. "Hello, Jenny. I'm so glad Ellen caught you before you left. I suggested you as my partner, since we work so well together."

I forced a smile, but inside, the acid in my stomach was churning. "Thank you, Braydon."

I turned to Ellen. "May I see the script?"

The older woman handed me a stapled packet. "Of course."

Once I'd read through the scene a couple of times, Ellen asked us to use the two chairs in the room as props. "By the way," she said, "you'll notice that I didn't put any actions or body language into the directions. That's intentional. I want to see how you interpret the lines."

My character's name was Amy and Braydon's was Mack.

Braydon began. "Amy, we've been together for three years. Don't you think it's time to decide what we're doing here?"

I shrugged. "If you say so, Mack. I still don't know why you want to force the issue. Things are fine the way they are."

He stood up and paced in front of my chair. "Because people keep asking. They want to know if we're getting married and having kids. I'm tired of living in limbo. Do you, or do you not, want to continue this relationship?"

"I'm just not sure yet." I looked down at floor. "Can we talk about this later? I have things to do."

He laid his meaty hand on my shoulder. "Come on. We've avoided the conversation long enough."

I subtly changed position enough for his hand to fall off my shoulder. "Of course, we have to talk about it sometime soon. I just have lot of work to do right now. I need to focus."

"That's what you always say." He sat down in the chair next to me.

I stood up and crossed my arms. "Okay, fine. What exactly are we discussing?"

He grabbed my hand. "Don't be daft. You know exactly what needs to be said."

I pulled my hand away and took a step back from his chair. "I do?" I moved further away from him.

He got up and followed me.

Revulsion hit me hard as he wrapped his arms around my waist and looked down at me. The acrid smell of sweat lingered in the air.

Wriggling out of his grasp, I said my next line. "I'm not ready to make a decision at this time."

"And scene!" Ellen clapped her hands.

I breathed a huge sigh of relief. I couldn't wait to leave.

"That was so interesting!" Ellen looked at us and that down at her script. "It was clear to me that Braydon's character wanted to stay together and get married. And Jenny's character didn't want to be in the relationship at all."

That was accurate. Both Amy and I didn't want anything to do with either Mack or Braydon.

"Can you try it again, but reverse the body language?" Ellen pointed to the first page. "Jenny, you try being more affectionate with Braydon—and Braydon, be standoffish. Let's see what that looks like."

*  *  *

Seven approaches of the scene later, Ellen clapped her hand and pointed. "That's it! I love it. Thank you so much for your work."

I was free. I wanted to run back to my dorm and take a hot shower so I could rinse Braydon's smell off me. He'd been constantly touching me—even when Ellen told him to act distant and cold. His sweat dried on my skin. I felt used and dirty.

I slung my backpack on my shoulder and practically dashed out the door of the rehearsal room.

As soon as I reached the outdoors, I took in a deep breath and let it out.

The sun had just begun its descent. The faint pink glow of the sky tickled the edges of the billowy, white clouds.

My eyes skirted around Washington Square Park. Was there a way for me to avoid walking by the big tree or the arch? I checked the time. It was after six o'clock. If I had any hope of getting some decent food before the dinner crowd demolished it, I had to take the shortcut, diagonally, through the grass. Avoiding the tree and the arch was not an option.

Running would get me there faster. I took off at a slow pace, letting my backpack bump against my back as I ran.

"Jenny!" I heard Braydon shouting. "Wait up!"

I pretended not to hear.

Behind me, I heard huffing and puffing as the large man attempted to catch up to me.

I remembered what I'd decided about strategy. Dang. I stopped and turned around.

"Didn't you hear me?" His rasping breaths grated on my nerves. He came to a full stop when he reached me.

"Sorry." I began walking in the direction of the dorm again. "I'm really hungry. I need to get to the cafeteria before they run out of food."

"I'll eat with you." His statement was just that. He'd declared his intentions, and I was supposed to follow along.

"I'm just grabbing some food and heading back to my room to study." I walked a little faster.

He made a grunting noise but didn't say anything else.

Before we got to the entrance, he passed me and opened the door for me. "After you."

I raised an eyebrow. "Thanks."

As soon as I stepped into the cafeteria, Braydon cleared his throat. "What are you doing this weekend?"

I closed my eyes and resisted the urge to bang my head against the wall. "My boyfriend is coming to visit, so I'll be with him and a couple of other friends who are also visiting."

He grunted. "I guess I'll see you around then."

"Maybe." I rushed to pick out my food. Luckily, they still had the taco bar set up, and I scrambled to assemble my food in a takeout container.

Once I'd made it through the cashier line, I looked back.

Braydon was sitting with a group from our morning acting class. None of them looked too pleased he had joined them.

I felt good that maybe his outing of me as a psychic hadn't done him any favors with our classmates. But immediately after thinking that, I felt a pang of guilt. Was I terrible person for wishing others wouldn't listen to him?

Walking up the stairs to my room, I realized that it wasn't that I didn't want other people to like him. I just didn't want Braydon to talk about my gift as a way to have leverage over me. He was using my fear of being outed as a psychic to make me agree to date him. No matter how I felt about my gift and people knowing about it, he was in the wrong.

I couldn't allow him to intimidate me. I needed to take my power back.

# Chapter 14

Back in my room, I pushed around my taco with a plastic fork. The situation with Braydon was putting me in a very bad mood.

In fact, I was convinced he had stolen the fun of my freshman year from me. He'd made me paranoid about people finding out who I really was. A psychic. A weirdo.

Feelings of self-doubt roiled through me. It was eerily similar to the feelings I'd had as a junior in high school—when my gift had lost me friends. I thought I'd gotten over all of that.

I guess I hadn't.

For the hundredth time, I wished I was just a normal college freshman. A student who was excited to be in a new city with new friends and new experiences to look forward to. Instead, I was constantly looking over my shoulder, wondering what people thought of me or if they'd avoid me because of my strangeness.

Cassandra burst in through the door and threw her backpack on her bed. "Hey, roomie!"

She took one look at my face, and instantly, her demeanor changed. "What's wrong? Did someone die?"

I sighed. I wasn't quite ready to share my true feelings. "No. I'm upset because Braydon won't leave me alone. He keeps asking me out even though I've told him over and over that I have a boyfriend. Honestly, even if he was the last man left on the planet, I still wouldn't date him."

"Even if the species would die out?" Cassandra grinned.

"Especially if the species would die out. I wouldn't want to create a bunch of little Braydon Dudeks to repopulate the world."

Cassandra let out peal of laughter. "I can just picture it…" She mimed a movie camera screen with her hands. "And there's little Braydon the third, out playing D&D with Braydon the fourth, fifth, sixth, and seventh."

I laughed. "Stop it. That's not making it any better."

She sat down on her bed. "Why do you think he won't take no for an answer?"

I shrugged. "I have no idea. This has never happened to me before. And I've never met anyone like him. It's almost as if the word 'no' is not in his vocabulary."

"Somehow, you'll need to figure out his currency. What will it take to make him understand?"

"Who knows?" I set my taco aside on the desk.

"Are you going to eat that?" She eyed the takeout container.

"No. Help yourself."

"Thanks!"

I watched in amusement as the taco disappeared in seconds.

Cassandra threw the container into the garbage and then looked up at me. "What else is bothering you?"

Damn. When had she become so perceptive? I paused a moment before I answered, not quite sure if I was ready to talk about it.

I took a deep breath and let it out. "I guess I'm still worried everyone will find out I'm psychic. I thought I'd moved past the anxiety of people knowing who—or what—I am. But when Braydon told all the students in our acting class, I got worried about how it will affect the way people interact with me."

Her mouth dropped open. "Are you serious? Why should you care what others think?"

I raised my eyebrows. "Don't most people care what others think about them?"

She frowned. "If they do, they shouldn't. And Jenny, of all people, you should know better. You have this incredible gift. You have insight that goes way beyond the normal range most people have. Don't you realize how special that is? How lucky you are?"

I felt shame color my cheeks. But, also a little anger. I stood up. She didn't know the terror of it. She didn't have any concept of the restless nights I'd experienced—drenched in sweat, dreaming of killers and victims. "You have no idea what it's like to have this gift. It makes me different. It separates me from others. It causes me emotional pain."

"But that's a good thing," Cassandra insisted. "I mean, not the pain, but the things you can do as a result. That makes you special."

"No! It makes me an outsider. Not only that, it keeps me from sleeping. It gives me nightmares—only the nightmares are real. It's terrifying. How would you like that, Cassandra? To be plagued with knowing things about people that you can't unknow? To see things you can't undo? To be unable to stop bad things from happening? To feel the pain when a madman breaks a victim's arm—to feel the *actual* pain, both physical and emotional, that the victim suffers? Sometimes, I hate that I have it. I didn't ask for this."

She shook her head. "I don't understand. How can you not see that you were meant to have this incredible gift? A talent that gives you the ability to *help* people." She picked up her backpack.

The look of disappointment in her eyes hit me like a punch to the gut.

She made a throaty noise that sounded a lot like a mother who'd just punished a disobedient child. "I'm going to the common room to study."

The door closed a little too loudly behind her.

I stood, stunned.

Tears brimmed in my eyes and spilled onto my cheeks.

Cassandra, the most positive and bubbly person in the world—the person who never said a bad thing about anyone, had just blown up at me. Me. Was I really such a horribly ungrateful person? I was no angel, I knew that. I wasn't perfect—not even close. But I was human. I had struggles, just like everyone else. Wasn't I allowed to express my fears? Why was she coming down on me so hard?

I sank onto the bed with my elbows on my knees and my head in my hands. I thought I'd felt alone before—but not like this. It was so much worse knowing that the one person who never judged me was deeply disappointed in me.

What had I done to make her so angry? Clearly, I had a lot of work to do to fix how I felt about myself and my gift. How could I make her realize that I knew my abilities were a good thing, but it also came with a lot of bad stuff? I had no idea how to explain it without it sounding like a pity party. The anxiety in me bubbled up, and I couldn't just wave a magic wand to make it go away.

*"Jenny."*

I lifted my head. Was Cassandra back already?

A woman with long dark hair was sitting next to me on my bed. She was wearing a floor-length, flowy white dress.

I crab-crawled backward on my bed, my spine hitting the headboard with a thud. I pulled my legs to my chest protectively. "Who are you?"

She put her hand out and touched my foot. *"My name is Isla. I'm your spirit guide."*

"My spirit guide?" My breathing was shallow and I felt lightheaded.

She smiled. *"I know you and Celine talked about spirit guides. She told you that everyone has at least one. You have three. The others wanted to come, but I didn't think we should overwhelm you. I chose to come alone."*

My mind spun. I wasn't sure what to do or say.

*"I want to help you release your fears."* She sat still, waiting for me to respond.

Still shaken from her sudden appearance, I wasn't quite sure how to respond. But the thought of having someone to help me gave me comfort.

"Thank you." I relaxed my shoulders.

*"I want to acknowledge your fears. They are valid."* She smiled. Her dark eyes were kind. *"But you should know that your guides are here for you. We are here to protect you to the best of our ability and offer advice or to listen when you need to talk."*

I frowned. "Protect me like the angels do when a dark entity is after me?"

She chuckled. *"Not quite. Angels are God's special beings who protect you and bring His light to you. They aren't human and never were. Whereas most spirit guides have lived at one time. We know what it's like to be human and what it's like to have fears and insecurities. We are here to guide you on your true path."*

Isla touched my arm, and I was surprised that the touch felt real—not like the touch of a ghost, which was ice cold. *"But, Jenny, you can't live your true path if you are bound in fear. Not wanting to be different is natural. However, as you know, you are far more critical of yourself than others are of you."*

I nodded.

She continued. *"If you are true to yourself and your path, others will recognize that and be more comfortable around you. Just be who you are. If they want to know more, they will ask. If they don't, let them be. They are on their own journey."*

Her words resonated with me. I felt the tension drift away. I was supposed to be me and let others be themselves. I hesitated. "I have so many questions."

*"I know."* Isla smiled.

Thinking of the way Cassandra and I had argued, I said, "How do I make people understand how my ability isn't all fun and exciting?"

*"Your friend Cassandra is a wonderful person. But she has trouble seeing how your gift frightens you—how it makes you wish you didn't have it at times."*

"Exactly!" I leaned forward. "I've tried so hard to explain it, but I'm not getting through her positivity bubble."

She laughed. *"I can help. We don't generally do this, but I will work as a conduit between you and Cassandra. The next time you try to explain to her what you're feeling, I will link you—so when she touches you, she can feel it too."*

"You can do that?" I thought of the hundreds of times I'd wished I could make people understand.

*"Yes. But, as I said, it's not something we do on a regular basis. I obtained special permission from the council to extend this."*

"The council?" I scooted a little closer to her.

*"The council is our own judicial board. As spirit guides, we may appear before the council to make a plea against a course we feel is detrimental to our charge's path."*

I furrowed my brows. "Huh?"

*"For example,"* Isla continued, *"say that my charge is in a dire situation and something happens that could*

*threaten what they were supposed to learn in this lifetime. I could go to the council and ask that their path be modified, so they could stay on their true course. Does that make sense?"*

I wrinkled my nose. "Kind of?"

She laughed. *"To be more succinct, spirit guides can ask the council's permission to alter your path so that you may learn the lessons you are here to learn."*

"I guess I get it. Thank you." I eyed the woman sitting next to me. She looked like she was from another century, with her long dress and her hair twisted back by her temples and the rest cascading down in ringlets. "You said most spirit guides have lived a life before? When were you alive?"

Her fingers straightened the fabric of her dress. *"I was alive from 1801 to 1860 in the country of Scotland. I also had a previous life in Greece many years before."*

I took that in. "You were reincarnated?"

She nodded. *"Yes. Each time a soul comes to life in the flesh, we are furthered on our path of spiritual evolution."*

"Will you be reincarnated again?" This was something I'd never really thought about—the ability to come back to life after one life was over.

Isla shrugged. *"Perhaps. If I feel the need to take another big step forward in my development, I may do so."*

Another question popped into my mind. "If you're my spirit guide, then you probably know that I'm having an issue with a classmate who won't leave me alone."

*"You're speaking of Braydon Dudek,"* Isla said promptly.

"Yes!" I was ecstatic that I was about to receive the answer I needed to deal with my Braydon problem.

*"I'm very sorry I can't help you with this. It is something you were meant to solve on your own."*

The air left my lungs, leaving me feeling deflated. "You can't even give me a hint?"

She chuckled. *"No. I know he annoys you. He annoys us too. But the problem you are having with him does not warrant a plea to the council. The problem you are having with Cassandra does warrant a plea, because it directly affects your ability to use your gift. Cassandra is meant to assist you in your work, and if she doesn't understand how your ability affects you as a person, she will not be able to do the work she is meant to do."*

I let that sink in. "This is weird. It almost sounds like we each have jobs—ones that were predetermined before we even met. But that can't be right."

Isla nodded. *"Yes, that is right. You both have your missions in this life. And here you are. Both of you have work that is vital and important. You need each other to fulfill your purpose here. You are to help people fight the evil and the darkness in this world. You are lightworkers."*

I'd never heard that term before. "Lightworkers?"

*"Yes. Living individuals who use their ordained power for the good of humanity. There are healers, psychics, and mediums, and more. Lightworkers are the means in which the spirit world can help man. Your channels of communication are open to us. In this way, we may spread light to those who need it. You are a gift to us as well as a gift to living people."*

I was silent. This was all too much.

"Okay," I finally said. "So, you'll help me make Cassandra understand?"

She nodded. *"All you have to do is touch her when you want her to experience what you're seeing."* She then went from solid to transparent, until she faded away completely.

# Chapter 15

Cassandra still wasn't back by the time I decided to go to bed. I was anxious to talk to her about Isla, but I was too tired to stay awake.

I sat on my bed and with half-closed eyes, looked out the open window at the park below. The wind had picked up, ruffling the blinds and the sheer, blue curtains fringing the window frame. I watched the clouds cover the stars and the moon and sighed. Autumn was on its way.

I gazed at the tree—the hanging tree—where we'd seen the form of a woman dangling from one of the branches. There was no woman now. I closed the window and shade to block out the lights and noise of the city before I snuggled down into the bed.

*The digital clock on the dashboard flashed three o'clock in the morning.*

*Her shift was ending in just a few minutes.*

*I'd parked in the loading zone close to the building. My eyes skimmed the front and lingered on the sign—New York Presbyterian/Lower Manhattan Hospital.*

*This time I wasn't taking any chances. She would be mine the moment she stepped out of the sliding glass doors.*

My eyes popped open. With a racing heart, I glanced at the clock on my desk. It was two o'clock in the morning.

Wait. In the dream, it'd been three o'clock when the man was waiting for the woman.

Did that mean...

I scrambled out of bed. If I hurried, I'd have time to stop him before he took her.

Cassandra was sprawled out on her bed, snoring lightly. I shook her shoulder. "Cassandra, wake up."

Her arm flailed out and smacked my chest. "Pizza does *not* grow on trees," she said with conviction.

"I know. Please, wake up!" I shook her again. "It's an emergency."

She groaned and rolled over onto her stomach.

My heart pounded faster. What should I do? I didn't want to go alone.

If I were home, I'd call Detective Coalfield...

I grabbed my phone and scrolled through my contacts until I found Detective Jeff Caruso. Without hesitation, I touched the number on the screen.

It rang a few times before a sleep-addled voice answered. "Detective Caruso."

"Detective, hi, it's Jenny Crumb. So sorry to bother you in the middle of the night, but there's a woman in extreme danger. She'll be kidnapped at three o'clock this morning, so we don't have much time."

"Is this what you were talking about when you asked about missing women in the area?" he asked.

"Yes. Remember, I said a man was taking three women? This is the third."

"Well, I checked into that, and no women fitting your description are reported missing."

My patience was wearing a little thin. The minutes were ticking away, and soon, there wouldn't be any time left to save the woman.

"I understand, Detective, but my vision was clear. There must be some reason I'm seeing what I'm seeing. We need to save this lady and stop the man who's about to do something awful to her and to the others he's taken."

"Tell you what," he said. "I can't send a team out there with absolutely no way to verify the information you've given. But, you and I can go check it out together. I'll pick you up in front of your dorm. Please tell me you know her location." His voice betrayed his suspicion of what I'd told him.

"She works at New York Presbyterian/Lower Manhattan Hospital."

"That's near you."

"Yes." I slipped on my shoes. "Maybe we can get there in time."

"See you in twenty minutes," he said before he hung up.

I tried one last time to wake Cassandra. "Cassandra!"

"Rumpelstiltskin is my name. Spinning gold, that's my game," she muttered before rolling over onto her side.

I rolled my eyes even though she couldn't see me.

Twenty minutes later, I'd slipped out the door and locked it behind me.

Detective Caruso pulled up to the curb just as I got to the sidewalk. "Great timing." I slid into the passenger seat of his unmarked car.

"Traffic is light." His dark hair was still rumpled from sleep, and his normally clean-shaven face was darkened by a night's growth of stubble.

I noted that he seemed grumpy—but I guessed it wouldn't be easy being awakened at this hour. Especially if he didn't think the threat was real.

"I'm sorry I woke you. But I do feel this is urgent."

He grunted and sped through a yellow light.

We approached the hospital slowly, from the back side of the building.

I closed my eyes and conjured up the image from my dream. I'd seen the sign—so, the front of the building.

I glanced at the time on the car's dash panel. It was three o'clock. "Can you drive around to the front doors?"

"Sure." He drove cautiously, like he was about to sneak up on somebody.

The streetlights lit the dirty beige façade of the hospital, which looked older and less remarkable than the surrounding buildings.

The loading zone in front of the hospital was empty.

"He should be here any minute now," I said.

Detective Caruso parked in a vacant handicapped spot kitty corner to the building, where we were somewhat hidden, but could see the entrance clearly.

A few seconds later, an older white van turned onto the street. It parked in the loading zone.

"There! That's him." I scooted forward to the edge of the seat. "He's waiting for her."

I hoped we were far enough away that the man wouldn't notice us. His engine was idling, as if he was ready to drive away the moment he grabbed her.

"Watch the front. I'm going to run the plates." The detective opened the small police-issued laptop he kept on the console between our seats. He keyed in the license plate number and waited.

"Here she comes." The door opened, and I watched in near panic mode as the woman I recognized from my dream stepped outside.

"Stolen plates." Detective Caruso said. "I'm calling it in." He quietly opened his door. Before he could slip out, the woman was suddenly joined by two large men who were also wearing scrubs.

The three of them chatted as they walked toward a vehicle parked in a spot marked "Reserved for Physicians Only."

On an impulse, I dug my phone out of my pocket and took a picture of the woman—though I had to zoom in quite a bit.

The man in the white van pounded his steering wheel and started the engine. He peeled off in the opposite direction, leaving behind a billowing cloud of exhaust.

Detective Caruso looked at me, his eyes wide. "You are definitely on to something, Jenny." He pressed a button on his dash. "All points bulletin on a white van, headed northeast on Beekman." He rattled off the license plate numbers and mentioned that the plates were stolen.

"Hang on." He floored the accelerator and we rocketed after the van.

The detective rolled down his window and stuck a flashing police light to the roof and turned on the siren.

I held my breath—thrilled that we were after a man I knew to be very, very bad, but also terrified. What if we caught him, but he wouldn't tell us where the women were being held? My guess is that they wouldn't be discovered, and they'd die alone. Their families would never know what had happened to them.

The van careened across two lanes and turned down a narrow, one-way street going the wrong way.

Detective Caruso cursed and made the hasty turn. Just as the van exited the road, another vehicle, who'd correctly turned onto the one-way street, blocked our way.

We came to a screeching halt, brakes squealing and siren blazing.

"Damn it!" the detective muttered.

The car, with its headlights blinding us, slowly backed out of the narrow street, allowing us to drive through.

By the time we exited, the white van was long gone.

My heart was thudding hard in my chest. We'd lost him!

I turned to Detective Caruso. "You have to warn that woman. He won't stop until he gets her."

He frowned. "I need to find her."

I held my phone and texted him the photo. "Now you have a picture. When you find her at the hospital tomorrow, ask her about the man who almost grabbed her while she was walking home the other night. She's already being more careful. Now she knows to take it a step further."

# Chapter 16

I tiptoed into the room and locked the door behind me. Cassandra was still on her stomach, snoozing.

I desperately wanted to tell her everything that'd happened during the night, but she was in a deep sleep. From previous experience, I knew she didn't wake up when she wasn't ready.

Sitting on the edge of the bed, I slipped off my shoes. It was four-thirty in the morning. With only three hours left before class started, I realized I had to at least try to get some sleep. I burrowed myself under the blankets and closed my eyes.

Once I'd rolled onto my side, the full force of exhaustion took over and I fell asleep.

*Their whispering voices echoed off the concrete walls.*

*I approached them and put my finger to my lips.*

*"Quiet!" I gave them a stern look.*

*Their frightened faces were pale in the light of the candle.*

*I needed to soothe them. "It's all right, girls. I'm here. Everything is going to be wonderful. You'll see."*

*I dipped the rag into the bucket of holy water. "Women need to be kept clean. Our vessels are given to us by God. We must not abuse or misuse our heavenly vessels, right?"*

*The thinner one whimpered.*

*"Shh. Shh. Hope, my sweet, you're fine." I ran the wet cloth lovingly across her cheek. Shh. Doesn't that feel nice?"*

*Tears ran down her face.*

*Delightful! She was crying with joy. I shifted the metal cuff on her wrist, stretched high above her head. The chain rattled as I washed her slender arm.*

*"You're beautiful, darling Hope. Just beautiful."*

*Faith began to sob.*

*"Oh, oh, dear Faith. I haven't forgotten about you." I rushed to her side and began to wash her body. See? That's better."*

*Faith hung her head low. I put a finger under her chin and tilted her face up to me. "I know you're anxious for our wedding day. But we have to wait for Charity to arrive. I'm so sorry I couldn't bring her to us tonight. I tried, I really did. I promise, I will bring her tomorrow. Then we will be married in the eyes of our Savior."*

My eyes popped open, and a choked scream escaped my lips.

"Jenny?" Cassandra whispered. "What happened?"

I put my hand to my chest and waited for my heart to stop hammering. Remembering what Isla had told me, I motioned for my friend to come sit on my bed.

"Cassandra. Remember how we argued about my gift?"

Confusion furrowed her brows. "Yes. But what does that have to do with your nightmare?"

"Would you like to know what this dream was about?"

She perked up. "Of course." She sat down next to me.

"There's a way that I can show you what's it's like. But I want you to be prepared. It might scare you." I searched her eyes for confirmation.

"I'll be fine."

I reached for her hand.

The moment I touched her, I felt the connectivity between us—the transferring of the experience. The dream replayed in my mind, and I knew she was undergoing the same thing I was.

Her eyes grew wider with each second and the color drained from her face. "What? What is this?"

I waited until the dream ended and let go of her trembling hand.

111

For once, she was quiet.

"Are you okay?" I asked.

Moonlight streamed through the slats of the blinds, highlighting her alabaster skin. Even her freckles had paled. "How did you do that? What did I just see?"

Immediately, I felt a pang of guilt. I shouldn't have sprung this on her without a full explanation. "Remember… remember the argument we had just before you left to study?"

She nodded, looking glum. "I'm sorry I was so hard on you."

"No. It was my fault. Sometimes I get so caught up in the things I see and feel—I forget that you don't understand what it's like." I looked down at my hands. "Last night after you left, a woman came to me. She sat right there where you're sitting—and she was solid. Like a real person."

Cassandra looked up at me, her brown eyes full of wonder. "Who was she? How did she get into our room?"

I leaned forward. "She told me she's my spirit guide. Her name is Isla."

Cassandra sprang to her feet, excited. "Get out! Seriously?"

I nodded, relieved she was into it. "Yeah. She said I have three spirit guides, but she didn't want the others to overwhelm me, so she came alone."

My friend sat back down. "Three? Wow. That's so cool." She paused for a moment. "What else did she say?"

"She said that you and I are meant to work together to help people."

Cassandra's eyes nearly bugged out of her head. "Really?"

"And the only way we could do that was if you could see what I see and feel what I feel."

"Wow," she whispered. "So—that's what that was? I saw what you saw?"

"Yes. All I have to do is touch you when I want you to connect with what I'm experiencing. By doing that, we'll be able to work together more closely."

"Holy crap. That's a lot to take in." She ran her fingers through her curls. "Do we both have to put our career plans on hold to help humanity or something?"

I laughed. "I didn't ask that, but I hope not. I figure that this is something we can do on the side while we pursue what we want to do in life."

"Yeah. That sounds good. I don't want to give up my art."

"You should never give up on that." I remembered the sketches she'd recently done while we were in Europe. They were incredible.

She seemed to absorb everything I'd told her. Then she said, "I want to hear all about that creepy dream again. Start from the beginning—but don't touch me. Just *tell* me this time."

\*\*\*

It was super hard to get up when our alarms went off. We'd stayed up apologizing to one another and talking about how we would use our new connection in the future.

"Normally, I don't need caffeine to wake up." Cassandra inspected the circles under her eyes in the mirror. "But today, I need a triple shot latte or whatever. I think we only got like an hour of sleep."

I groaned and joined her in front of the mirror. "Ugh. Me too. I need caffeine and lots of makeup to cover up my puffy eyes." It didn't help that I'd been crying after our fight the previous night. But now that we'd reached an understanding, I was feeling much, much better.

My phone buzzed. It was Benny.

"Hey, girl! Frank and I are flying in to NYC today."

113

"What? Today? I thought you were coming next week." The time had gone by so fast. Maybe I'd gotten my dates wrong.

"Sorry. I should've told you. Frank rearranged our travel plans a bit because some of his military buddies are in town."

"Do you want to meet up tonight?" I asked.

"No. We won't be able to hang out until Friday night. We're visiting Ithaca first, then Columbia, NYU, and Pace on Thursday and Friday. Then we're flying home on Sunday."

"That's not a lot of time to visit," I said, feeling a little disappointed. "But at least we have the whole weekend together."

"Didn't you say Mike was coming to visit as well?" he asked.

"Yep. We'll have a mini-reunion! It'll be fun."

"Are you sure you don't want to just spend a romantic weekend alone with your boyfriend?" His voice was hesitant.

"Of course I want to spend time with Mike. But you're just as important to me. Mike's only a couple hours away, while you're like three thousand miles from here. I can see Mike any time."

"Okay, good. I just didn't want to be a third wheel. Should I just text you Friday so we can make plans?"

"Yeah, that sounds great. Can't wait to see you, Benny."

"Back at ya," he said.

We hung up, and I finished putting on my makeup. "That was Benny."

"I figured as much." Cassandra grinned and tied her shoes. "Sounds like we're hanging out this weekend?"

"Uh huh. Start thinking of stuff we might want to do in the city. We need to impress him so he'll choose NYU when it's time to apply for schools."

"Easy peasy." Cassandra opened the door. "New York City is the coolest place in the world. He'll love it here."

# Chapter 17

"You got mail." Cassandra bounced into our room waving an envelope. "Guess who it's from?"

I looked up from my homework and reached for it.

"Nope." Cassandra pulled it away from my outstretched hand. "You have to guess."

I sighed and rested my hands in my lap. "My mom and dad?"

"Wrong." Her eyes twinkled and the corner of her mouth twitched.

"Uh, Mike?" But why would Mike write me a letter? He could just text me.

"Wrong." She waggled her eyebrows. "Guess again."

"Oh, come on." I stood up and snatched the letter from her hand.

"No fair!" Cassandra screeched and tried to take it from me.

"Oh, no you don't." I spun away. "You've had your fun." I read the address on the top. "It's from the NYPD."

"I bet it's your paycheck." Cassandra grinned.

My mind whirled with excitement and anxiety. I guessed that the police didn't pay consultants a ton. But I hadn't a clue how much would be inside the envelope.

I held my breath and gingerly opened it, careful not to tear what was inside. I pulled out the check and a folded piece of paper behind it. I read the amount and smiled. "It's five hundred dollars."

"Sweet!" Cassandra high-fived me. "That's five hundred you can deduct from your bill. What's in the paper underneath?"

I unfolded it. "It's a note from Detective Caruso. It says, "Jenny, thank you for helping us to solve not one, but two crimes. Your expertise is invaluable. I'm sorry we can't pay more at this time, though I suspect your paychecks will increase the longer you work for us. FYI, I checked with Andrew Carver's family, and they were extremely grateful for your help in finding their son. Mrs. Carver wanted to do something special for you, so she wrote you the enclosed check. Looking forward to working with you again soon. Sincerely, Detective Jeff Caruso.""

I blinked. Mrs. Carver had given me money? It was facedown inside the folded paper. I turned it over. My breath caught in my throat.

"Jenny, you've gone pale." Cassandra's brows furrowed. "What is it?"

"You know that little boy I helped find? The one that a kidnapper almost took?"

She nodded. "Yeah."

"His mother wanted to reward me for finding him." I held up the check. My heart skipped at least two beats. "Two thousand dollars."

"OMG!" Cassandra jumped up and down. "You can pay off that bill. And you have five hundred left over. I'm so excited for you!"

I thought my grin would split my entire face in half. "This is amazing. I can't believe it." But then my stomach dropped. Should I be taking money from someone for doing a good deed?

"What's the matter?" Cassandra asked. "Aren't you happy?"

"Sure. Do you think it's okay for me to take their money?" The doubt I'd been feeling rose up into my throat.

"Jenny, you told me that they're a wealthy family. They are so grateful you saved their son. Let them do something nice for you. You'd be insulting them if you returned it." Cassandra patted my arm.

The doubt receded. "Maybe you're right."

"Of course I'm right, girlfriend. March yourself right down to the ATM machine, deposit that money, and pay off your bill at the financial aid office. This will be a huge weight off your shoulders." She grabbed my arm. "Come on. I'll go with you."

***

Cassandra was right. A weight had definitely lifted off my shoulders. I felt light as air.

"Let's go celebrate. I say, we go out for some of that famous New York City pizza. What do you think?"

"Sounds great. Should we invite April?"

"Oh, for sure." Cassandra sent a text to our friend. A second later, her phone buzzed. "Ooh, she's quick. She'll meet us at Wasquapa in five minutes. She says she's starving."

"That makes two of us." My stomach rumbled.

"Three of us." Cassandra dragged me down the sidewalk to the edge of the park.

"Hello, ladies." The unmistakable voice of Braydon Dudek came from behind us.

The air whooshed out of my lungs. I turned to face him. "Braydon." I tried not to let the sourness I was feeling creep into my voice. I failed.

118

He was wearing the same food-stained chinos as he wore the day before. His two-sizes-too-small t-shirt strained against his doughy chest. "Where are you headed?" Cassandra put her hands on her hips, as if to challenge him. "Out to dinner."

Braydon glanced at his phone. "Mind if I tag along? I'm hungry, and I need to get a quick bite to eat before my voice lesson at six-thirty."

I faked a frown. "Oh, I'm sorry. We're going to the theatre district. I don't think you'd get back in time to get to your lesson."

Cassandra looked at me and raised one eyebrow. "Yeah, we're going to catch the subway in. It's rush hour, so we'll be lucky to catch a train right away."

"Shoot. You're right. Not enough time. Catch you next time?" His gaze drifted to my chest.

I turned away. "Maybe. Have a good night, Braydon."

As soon as he was out of earshot, Cassandra said, "Do you believe that guy? He couldn't stop staring at your boobs."

"I know. I'm torn between punching him and worrying about being rude." I opened my purse and dug out a tube of Chapstick.

Cassandra stopped abruptly, color rising in her cheeks. "No. You cannot be worried about being rude. You were plenty patient with him when you first met him. He has consistently pushed and pushed you to go out with him, even though you've told him you're not interested. He's practically stalking you. No more being nice and worrying about hurting his feelings. Stand up for yourself."

I nodded. "You're right. I guess I was too nice because I've seen kids be really mean to people like Braydon. I always want to defend the underdog, you know?"

"Well, he's not an underdog. He's a hell hound. You need to stand up for yourself. And if that means you have to be rude to him, then so be it." She struck a boxing pose with her fists curled in front of her. "Let him have it next time."

I linked my arm through hers. "You're sassy. I like that."

"Well, I don't like that guy. He's a creep. Hey, look! There's April. Come on." She dragged me across the park diagonally.

April walked toward us at a clipped pace. "Where do you want to eat? I haven't had food since this morning."

"Jenny suggested somewhere that has New York City pizza," Cassandra said.

April shrugged. "I bet there's a pizza place on every block."

"I'd love to eat in the theatre district." My stomach grumbled loudly. "If we stay close to campus, we might run into Braydon again. I can't handle that right now."

"Gotcha." April headed toward the subway entrance. "I know a good place to eat over there. It's a little more upscale than plain old pizza. That okay with you?"

"Sounds great."

We walked down the stairs to catch the A train, April leading the way. The faint smell of stale urine scented the air as we descended deeper underground.

I didn't know if it was due to hunger, the disgusting odors, or the fact that we were in a tunnel that made my vision begin to blur. Was I slipping into a vision? The dirty concrete walls closed in on me.

*Flash.*
*Footsteps echoed in the distance.*
*"He's coming back," I hissed.*
*The other girl, Hope, sobbed. "No. What if he has her? What's he going to do to us?"*
*"Shhh. I don't know." I tried once more to slip my hands out of the metal bindings attached to the chain. "Try to keep calm."*

*Hope wailed. "I can't! I can't!" She was breathing too fast, spiraling into a panic attack.*

*"Shhh, Hope. Take deep breaths." It was ironic that I was trying to keep her calm when every particle of me wanted to scream, and scream, and scream.*

*His voice, honey-coated and purposely soft, sounded in the dark chamber. "Hello, lovelies. Did you miss me?"*

\*\*\*

"Are you serious?" April set soda down on the red and white checked tablecloth and stared at me. "You keep seeing this guy in your dreams, uh, visions or whatever?"

My hands shook as I reached for my glass of water. "Sometimes, I see through his eyes, but I've never gotten a good look at him."

April made a face. "That's so creepy."

The smell of oregano, bubbling cheese, and tangy tomato sauce hung in the air. Somehow, the fragrant scents, the sounds of clinking silverware, and people chatting nearby brought comfort to me.

I took in a deep breath and let it out. "Mostly, the visions come in dreams. This time though…" I shuddered, thinking about the fear I sensed from the women he held captive. "This time, the vision came as we went down the stairs to the subway. It pulled me under into the darkness."

"Then what?" Cassandra chewed her pizza, her eyes wide.

"I was underground somewhere. I could hear faint echoes, so it was somewhere with thick walls where the sound could bounce off them. Two women were there. I was one of them, seeing through her eyes. He hadn't arrived yet. We were chained to the wall. We were trying to slip out of the metal cuffs on our wrists, but then he came back."

Cassandra's lip quivered. "Did you see him?"

121

"No. Right after that, I came to. You guys were pulling me up off the stairs."

April pointed her fork at me. "But now, you've seen what one of the women look like. Do you think you could recognize her from a picture?"

I nodded. "Sure, but if there aren't any missing women reported in that area, where would I find the pictures to identify her?"

Cassandra perked up. "Didn't you tell me their names were Hope and Faith?"

I shrugged. "That's what he called them. Maybe he just made those names up. Don't you think their names sound religious? This whole thing is some kind of sick ritual for him."

"Those are the worst kind of crazies." April leaned forward. "The ones who use religion to do awful things."

"And the dumb thing is," Cassandra jumped in, "no religion would condone hurting others. It's the sick people who twist the teachings into something ugly, and then claim that God told them to do it."

"True. We see so many examples of that in the news. There are a lot of irrational people out there." My nerves had finally settled down enough so that my stomach was no longer twisted in knots. I took a bite of the pizza, which was still warm. It was delicious.

"Does this have anything to do with the visions you keep having in Washington Square Park? And the woman hanging in the tree?" April asked.

"I don't think so." I thought about the distinctive visions I'd had while crossing Wasquapa. "I don't see the women or the man who took them while I'm in the park. It's more like…" My eyes drifted toward the window where the endless stream of people walking by lulled me into deeper thought.

Cassandra and April waited patiently for me to collect my feelings.

I turned my attention back to them. "In the park, it feels like there are lots of lots of people. They're in the ground. Underneath. I feel their sorrow. Their disappointment in life and how it ended." I closed my eyes, trying to rid myself of the oppressive feelings from my visions.

April drank the last of her soda. "It sounds like you're saying that people are buried in the ground *under* the park."

I raised my eyebrows. "Yeah. That's what it feels like."

She got out her phone, did a quick search, and then gasped. "Guess what? You're right. There are people underground. Washington Square Park used to be a potter's field."

Cassandra wrinkled her nose. "Potters? Like people who make ceramics? What does that have to do with dead people?"

April giggled and pointed at her phone. "That's what I thought at first. But a potter's field is a term they used for a cemetery for poor people. Kind of a common grave of sorts."

I nearly choked on a bite of pizza. "What?"

Cassandra banged her hand down on the table. "Holy cow! That explains a lot!"

The people sitting next to us jumped. A guy sporting a goatee and a newsboy cap gave us the stink eye.

Our server rushed over. "Is everything okay?" she asked.

I took a sip of water and cleared my throat. "Sorry. We're good."

The corners of her mouth turned down slightly. "Okay. Let me know if you need anything."

I glared at Cassandra. "You're going to get us in trouble."

"Sorry." She blushed. "I got carried away. But, with all those dead bodies under your feet, it's no wonder you keep passing out in the park!"

123

April scrolled through the article on her screen. "It says here that the people buried in the field were the poor, indigent, criminals, and many were victims of the yellow fever epidemic. The site was used as a burial ground from 1797 through 1826."

I shuddered. "God. How awful."

"Plus, there were lots of churches in the area who had their own burial sites nearby." April put her phone in her pocket. "That's a lot of dead people."

"Sounds like there's a lot of misery in that spot. I bet you're picking up on it." Cassandra took her last bite of food and pushed her plate to the side.

I felt a sense of relief that what had happened there was back in the past and not some atrocity happening now.

As if she'd read my mind, Cassandra said, "Do you think the poor souls who were buried there have unfinished business? That might explain why you're having those visions."

Shrugging, I answered, "Maybe. Or maybe I'm just picking up the impressions and memories of what happened back then, and it's playing on a loop."

"Is that a thing?" April laid her napkin on her empty plate.

"Yep. Many places where people have claimed there's a haunting are actually just memories of bad things that happened there. Those moments play over and over, even though the souls of the people who died have long since moved on to the other side."

"That's wild." April flagged down the server, who looked none too pleased to be called to our table. "We're ready to pay. Can we get separate bills?"

"No, no." I held up my hand. "It's on me. I just got paid, and I want to do something nice for you both."

April grinned. "Thanks!"

Cassandra frowned. "Are you sure, Jenny?"

"Of course I'm sure. You guys keep pulling me off the ground when I see scary things. I owe you one."

After I paid the bill, we joined the throng of people heading every which way in the theatre district. Neon lights and billboards announcing the current offerings of Broadway shows lit up the dark sky.

Cassandra opened her arms out wide, tilted her head up, and spun in a slow circle. "This is the greatest city in the world! Don't you love it?" She grinned at us.

"You dork." April laughed. The two joined hands and spun around, giggling.

Several disgruntled passersby moved off the sidewalk to avoid collision with them.

I pulled out my phone and snapped some photos. "These are too good not to share. I'm posting these."

"You have to be in them too!" Cassandra grabbed my phone. "Selfies!"

Several minutes and about twenty pictures later, we finally headed back. We window shopped until our feet got tired, and then made our way below the street to catch a subway back to school.

The night had a chill to it as we resurfaced near Washington Square Park.

"Maybe we should avoid walking through there," Cassandra steered us to the outskirts of the square.

"Don't be silly." I grabbed her arm and pulled her toward the grass. "Now that I know what I'm seeing, I think I can ward off those visions. Come on. Let's run!"

The three of us squealed as we ran toward the arch at one end of the park. We made it to the other side, laughing hysterically. I looked back, wondering how many of our classmates had witnessed our childish behavior.

Then I saw it.

The figure of a woman hanging from the ancient elm tree, right where we'd seen her before.

125

# Chapter 18

"Why do you think we keep seeing that woman hanging in the park?" Cassandra unlocked the door to our room and swung it open.

April shook her head. "It's really disturbing."

I followed them inside. "There are so many possible reasons why she appears."

"Like what?" Cassandra took off her jacket and plunked down on her bed.

"Hanging was really common in those days. People were hanged for all kinds of things. Maybe this lady was accused of stealing or something and that was her sentence." I scooted the desk chair toward April and motioned for her to have a seat.

"And if she didn't do it, maybe her unfinished business is that she wants us to prove her innocence?" She settled into the chair.

"Could be," I said.

"Maybe it's something more than that." Cassandra tugged on an auburn curl. "What if she's trying to tell us something about the bodies in the potter's field?"

I nodded. "That's a possibility too. I feel really bad about those people. I wonder if their families knew they'd died. And if they did, where would they go to pay their respects? Were they buried in a mass grave or separate graves? I have so many questions."

"Can we try to talk to her?" April leaned forward in her chair. "We could go outside and stand in front of that tree. If she really wants to tell us something, she might just appear."

"That would be good," I said. "I mean, it rarely is that simple. Usually, I'm given little tidbits of information here and there until I finally piece it all together. But, I *have had* some interactions with spirits who are very good at communicating. It would be great if she was able to tell us what she wants."

Cassandra jumped to her feet. "Let's try it!"

"Now?" I glanced at my backpack. I still had homework to do.

"Yeah!" April stood up. "It will only take a few minutes."

I sighed. "Okay. But if we don't get anything right away, I want to come back here. I've got too much to do."

"Deal." Cassandra yanked the door open, and we headed down the stairs and out the front of the building.

The night air carried a chill. Clouds blew quickly by overhead as the wind picked up and whistled through the streets, as if the tall buildings were the walls of canyons.

Once we reached the tree, I could tell by the faces of my friends that they were nervous.

"Now what?" April stared up at the branches.

Cassandra turned to me. "Do we say something? Ask her to come out and play?"

Even though she was joking, I detected a slight tremor in her voice. I laughed to break the tension. "I have no idea."

We waited several minutes without speaking. The sounds of engines and sirens in the distance reminded me that we weren't all alone. Even if something scary happened, we were surrounded by people who could help.

127

"Maybe we should just go sit on that bench and have a regular conversation." April pointed to the one nearest us. "There might be too much pressure for her to appear if we're standing here staring at the tree."

We sat down on the bench and tried to hold a legit conversation.

The fingers brushing the hair off my shoulders from behind, made me jump. "Aagh!" I turned my head so fast, I nearly gave myself whiplash. "Braydon!"

His hands never left my shoulders. "Hello, girls. What are you doing in the park at night?"

I tried shrugging his hands away, but they were firmly planted.

April narrowed her eyes at him. "It's none of your business."

"Why so hostile?" he asked as he began massaging my shoulders.

I catapulted myself off the bench and turned to face him. "Actually, we were just leaving. Come on guys."

April and Cassandra looked at each other and then shot off the bench as quickly as I had.

"Yeah, I'll walk you back to your dorm," April said. She and Cassandra linked their arms through mine and we scurried through the front door of our building.

"Damn," Cassandra said once we got back to our room. "Braydon has crossed way over the line. Do you think we should report him?"

"To whom?" I sighed as I plunked down on my bed. "And what are we going to say? Braydon Dudek rubbed my shoulders and keeps asking me out?"

Cassandra shrugged. "I don't know. But maybe the administration can have a talk with him."

"Who would we tell? Campus police? The dean of the musical theatre department?" April asked.

Cassandra chewed on her lip. "I don't know. But we should tell somebody."

"Mike will be here soon. I'm really hoping Braydon will get a clue once he sees with his own eyes that I'm in a relationship. It'll be a lot more real to him once Mike is with me."

Cassandra frowned. "You've already told him multiple times. He knows you're in a relationship. He simply doesn't care."

I swallowed hard. "Yeah, you're right. Tell you what, if he does anything else in the next few days, I'll find a way to report him somehow."

She nodded. "Okay. He's getting way too bold. You've got to nip this in the bud before he does anything crazy."

The thought made me very uncomfortable. To report someone for intimidating me meant that he could be punished severely—or not at all. In either case, I shuddered to think what he would do to me if he discovered I'd turned him in. But if I didn't, what would he do if he came upon me while I was alone?

April opened the door. "I need to get back to my dorm. I've got too much to do." She touched her phone screen. "I'm texting campus security to walk me back. I don't want any run-ins with Braydon or any other creep for that matter."

I swallowed hard. "I'm so sorry. I feel like this is all my fault."

April gave me a meaningful look. "It's not your fault. You are doing everything you can to avoid this guy. He is the one who's at fault."

Once she'd left, I took a deep breath and settled on my bed. I wiped a tear off my cheek, and I got out the homework assignment from my backpack.

Cassandra pulled a journal off her little bookshelf. "I'm documenting every encounter you've had with Braydon. If he does anything else, I'm taking this to the administration."

I bit my lip. "Okay. Thank you."

I worked through my homework slowly while I tried to process the things that were happening.

Cassandra must have sensed my confusion and anxiety. "Focus on the good things. Mike and Benny will be here on Friday!"

My spirits lifted, and I smiled. "You're right. That's definitely something to look forward to."

Maybe Braydon would stay away from me once I had good men by my side.

## Chapter 19

When Friday afternoon arrived, I was anxious. I sat on the bench near the edge of the park, watching people walk by after class. The late afternoon had reverted back to summer weather. With not a cloud in the sky, the warm breeze ruffled the trees. I could almost imagine the sound the leaves would make if I could only hear them over the steady hum of traffic.

I scanned the surrounding area, waiting to catch a glimpse of Mike. He was supposed to arrive any minute.

In which direction would he be coming? There were a couple subway stops nearby. My eyes darted back and forth between the two possible streets he could emerge from.

I hadn't seen him since mid-August, and I was excited to spend time with him—especially in this environment far away from home.

I looked from right to left. What would he be wearing?

A tall guy in the distance caught my eye. The closer he got to the park, the more convinced I was it was him. Then, his face turned in my direction. It wasn't him.

Glancing at my phone, I realized I'd been waiting here for over twenty minutes. Where was he? I was about to text him when a figure in the distance made me take a second look.

Tall and fit, he was wearing jeans and a gray canvas jacket. He shifted the backpack from one shoulder to the other as he pulled out his phone.

My cell buzzed. "I'm near the park. Where should we meet?"

Ignoring the phone in my hand, I darted off the bench and ran toward him as fast as my legs could carry me. "Mike!" I waved my arms.

He stopped and looked up from his screen. He broke into a wide grin—the kind that always made me weak in the knees. "Jenny."

Once I reached him, he wrapped his arms around me, and I was lost in his embrace.

Finally, I pulled away and looked up into his green eyes. "It's so good to see you. I can't believe you're here—that *we're* here in New York City!"

He brushed a strand of hair off my shoulder. "I can't believe it either." He bent down to kiss me gently on the lips. "I'm just happy to spend the weekend with you."

My thoughts flicked momentarily to Benny, who we'd be meeting up with us later in the evening. Although I was dying to see him, I selfishly wanted to spend some time alone with Mike. I sighed. "You'll have to share me with Benny."

He laughed. "Good thing I like him. And good thing he isn't into girls."

I scowled at him in mock disappointment. "Would you be jealous of him if he was?"

"Maybe a little." He grabbed my hand and we walked toward my dorm building. "But I trust you, so maybe not so much."

I looked up at him with adoration. "I love you. You're the best."

He gave me a crooked grin. "Love you too."

Just as we approached the front of the building, the doors swung open. Braydon Dudek, in all his rumpled glory, stepped onto the sidewalk.

I inched closer to Mike and whispered, "Braydon."

Braydon blocked the doors with his large body. He gave us a nod. "Jenny."

"Hello, Braydon." I reached for the door handle.

He put up his arm to block me. "Wait a minute. You haven't introduced me to your friend."

Mike stuck out his hand, "I'm Mike. Jenny's *boyfriend*."

"Ah, so you're the mysterious Mike that Jenny keeps telling me about. I was beginning to think that you didn't exist and that she was making you up just to get rid of me."

"I can assure you," Mike said with tight smile, "that I'm quite real." His shoulders stiffened.

"So, I see." Braydon stepped away from the door, allowing us to pass. "Well, it was nice meeting you, Mike."

When we reached the top of the stairs, I let out the breath I'd been holding. "Thank God. Now he finally knows he needs to leave me alone."

Mike grunted. "That guy is an ass. There's something unsettling about him."

"Tell me about it." I opened the door with my key and went inside my room.

"If he so much as touches a hair on your head, I'll punch him." Mike set down his backpack and looked around the room. "This is nice. I like it."

My spirits lifted as the subject was changed. "It is. Cassandra should be here any minute. And Benny's arriving in an hour or so."

Mike smiled. "That gives us just a few minutes to get reacquainted." He pulled me to him and kissed me.

The door swung open. "Mike!"

April and Cassandra entered the room. April stood back and watched as Cassandra flung herself at him and hugged

133

him fiercely. "I'm so glad you're here." When she stepped away, she frowned. "Oh, I hope we weren't interrupting anything…"

"Not yet," I said with a smile.

Mike's cheeks flushed a little, which I thought was adorable. "I hear we're all hanging out this weekend. When is Benny arriving?"

I checked the time. "Any minute. Maybe we should figure out a place to eat dinner, so we can head out when he gets here." Nearly forgetting my manners, I realized that April and Mike had never met. "Mike, this is our friend, April."

"Nice to meet you." Mike shook April's hand.

Cassandra, still focused on food, grabbed her phone. "Do we want to eat somewhere around here? We could take the subway to the theatre district. Or maybe even Little Italy."

"And if we don't feel like eating Italian food, Chinatown is right next to that." My stomach grumbled.

Cassandra threw up her arms. "Who are we kidding? There are so many kinds of food to choose from. Let's just let Benny decide when he gets here."

We hung out in our room and chatted until my phone buzzed. "It's him. He's outside in front of the building."

"Let's go meet him!" Cassandra bounced off the bed, shoved her feet in her sneakers, and flung open the door.

Mike, April, and I trailed behind her as she flew down the stairs. When we stepped outside, Benny was standing on the sidewalk—but he wasn't alone. The guy standing next to him had tousled, sandy blond hair and twinkling blue eyes.

"Duncan!" Cassandra squealed and raced to throw herself at her handsome Scottish boyfriend. "What are you doing here?" Tears of joy ran down her cheeks.

He wrapped his arms around her and squeezed her tight. "Surprise! Benny and I have had this planned for a while now."

She laughed and wiped her face. "You guys are sneaky. But I'm so glad you're here!"

"What am I? Chopped liver?" Benny held out his arms, waiting for hugs.

I laughed and hugged him. "I missed you."

"I missed you too." Once he pulled away, he hugged everyone else.

Duncan, too, got hugs from us all, even Mike and April. Even though they'd just met, they were soon chatting like old friends.

"Where's Frank?" I asked. Frank had accompanied Benny to check out colleges. Benny had emancipated himself from his parents and Frank, a retired military officer whom we'd met during a workshop for psychics, had graciously taken Benny in.

"He's spending the next few days with his military buddies."

"I hope we get to see him before you guys head back," I said.

"I'll make sure of it." Benny looked up at the building. "Is this your dorm?"

"Yeah. Doesn't look anything like a dorm, does it? It's just another tall building. But we like it. We'll show you our room after dinner."

"Speaking of dinner," Cassandra said, "what do you guys feel like eating?"

"Food," Benny deadpanned.

Cassandra punched his arm. "Wise guy."

I grinned and watched my posse of friends. I was the luckiest girl in the world.

"Well, I don't know about you," Duncan said. "But I'm in the mood for some American food."

Cassandra exchanged a look with me.

"Come on, everyone. Shake Shack it is." Cassandra linked arms with Benny and Duncan and practically tugged them along.

I giggled as the image of Dorothy walking on the yellow brick road with the tin woodsman and the scarecrow popped into my head.

We headed through the park. As we passed the hanging tree, a slight shiver skittered over my skin.

I reflexively looked up at the sturdy branch once used for hangings, but there was nothing there.

## Chapter 20

After dinner and an off-off Broadway play, the temperature was still pleasant, in the low sixties. In the late hour, there wasn't as much activity in the park as I would've expected on a Friday night. But, there were little groups of students and city dwellers walking about, probably coming home from a fun night out.

As we were nearing Washington Square Park, it dawned on me that we'd be hosting three guests—and we hadn't made any plans to accommodate them.

"Oh, my God! Where is everyone going to sleep? I mean, we can maybe fit one on the floor, but..." My voice trailed off. This whole time, I'd imagined that Mike would stay in our room, but I hadn't thought about where Benny would stay. And now Duncan was in the mix too.

Benny stopped in his tracks. "You mean, I came all this way just to sleep on the street somewhere?"

"And what about me?" Duncan frowned. "I've come all the way from the UK."

Mike remained silent.

My heart sank. "I'm so sorry. I don't know what to do. Cassandra, maybe we can ask some of the people on our floor if they can take in a guest?"

The practiced blank stares from Mike, Duncan, and Benny caught me off guard. What were they up to? They were quiet only a few seconds before they burst out laughing.

"Gotcha!" Benny high-fived Duncan and Mike. The three of them laughed way too hard.

"Did you see her face?" Duncan covered his mouth with his hand.

Cassandra's eyebrows formed a deep V. "What in the world?"

April seemed just as confused as Cassandra and I were.

Benny snorted. "The three of us are staying in a hotel just a block away from here." He put his arm around my waist and hugged me close.

The tension left me, but now I was annoyed. "What? Why didn't you tell us?"

"Because of *that* reaction." Benny pointed to me and grinned. "It was gold."

"Benny, grow up. In fact, all three of you need to grow up." I glared at them.

"Don't be mad," Mike said. "We were just kidding around."

I shook my head. "Just remember, payback's a—"

Cassandra covered my mouth with her hand. "Don't say it." She whispered to me, "We'll get even later."

I was still slightly annoyed as we neared the hanging tree.

A breeze blew past my ears, and the cold seeped into my bones.

Oh, no. Was a vision coming? Or was it only the wind?

My friends had stopped walking and had focused their attention on the branch. *The* branch. The woman swung above us, her skirt fluttering back and forth.

Terror lit my friends' faces. My eyes darted to Mike. He'd never been able to see ghosts or spirits before, but he was clearly seeing the same thing I was.

138

The streetlights made a strange buzzing noise and wavered. The woman's body appeared to jerk with the flickering lights, as if she were lit up by a strange strobe light at a macabre Halloween party.

April and Cassandra whispered to each other, no doubt revisiting their theories about the hanging woman. The guys, however, were completely freaked out, their mouths hanging open in shock.

The street lights suddenly stuttered and fizzled out. The entire surrounding area went dark.

"Holy crap," I heard Benny mutter.

A passing garbage truck's headlights illuminated the darkness. The dead woman stood directly before us—her face a shade of gray, her eyes hollow. Angry red rope burns scored the delicate skin on her neck.

We were bathed in darkness once again as the truck rumbled past.

The woman still stood there. My eyes were adjusting to the dark, and she became more and more visible with each second that passed. Though, I was sure if I reached out to touch her, my hand would go right through her body.

"April," the woman croaked.

April took a step back. "Who? What?"

The woman motioned for us to follow her. She glided toward the intersection, which had recently been torn up for construction.

I looked at my friends, my heart pounding wildly. "She wants us to follow her. Come on."

"Seriously?" Benny hissed. "Is this a good idea?"

April whispered, "Probably not, but I'm going anyway." She was the first to bolt after the ghost, her dark curls bouncing as she ran to keep up.

When we got to the construction site, there was a deep hole in the corner where the street met the sidewalk. The ghost woman hovered over the hole and then slid downward into it.

I approached the hole and peered into the darkness.

"What are they doing construction on this corner for?" Duncan looked up at the building facing us. "There's no scaffolding. It's just construction on the sidewalk and this section of the street."

"There's one of those notices of construction projects over here." Benny peered at the sign. "It says they're replacing old pipes under the street."

Carefully, I wiggled my way past the barriers and into the opening of the street. I lowered myself down onto a chunk of concrete below.

"Jenny, what are you doing?" Benny asked. "You can't go down there. It's dangerous."

I shuffled forward a few steps and spotted an old board leaning against a cement wall. Pushing the board with my foot, it toppled off to the side. "There's a small doorway here." I ducked down and crawled through.

"Wait for me." April hopped down and crawled through behind me.

Soon, we were all semi-standing with our backs bent to keep from hitting our heads on the thick concrete above. Mike turned on his cell phone flashlight.

The light revealed dirty rock walls and a path wide enough for us to walk two-by-two.

"Yuck," Benny said. "It smells like urine, rats, and cockroaches down here."

"What is this? Part of the NYC underground?" Cassandra asked.

"You mean like the one underneath downtown Seattle?" A trickle of sweat rolled down my back. It was warmer here than on the street level. The air was stagnant and dank.

"New York City's underground is far more extensive than the one in Seattle," Cassandra said. "And they don't call it the underground here. They just refer to anything below street level as the subway."

Benny looked at her sidewise. "How do you know that?"

"I read, Benny," she said, rolling her eyes. "My interests cover a wide range of topics."

He grunted. "I'm not trying to be a smart ass. I just didn't think you knew about New York City geology or whatever, that's all."

"Not geology. History," Cassandra said. "NYC has a vast subway system. Lots of abandoned tunnels and what-not." She glanced back to the opening we ducked through. "And it doesn't appear as though the construction workers have discovered this one yet."

"Does that mean that we're the first to see this after maybe a hundred years or more?" April grinned.

"Maybe." Cassandra took a few steps forward. "Want to see what's down here?"

"But where did the ghost go?" Duncan asked. "I saw her slip into the street opening, but I didn't see her afterward."

As if the ghost had been listening to our conversation, she appeared further down the path, which angled downward like a ramp.

"There." Mike pointed. "She's motioning for us to follow."

April and Cassandra were the first to move ahead. Mike and Duncan were next. Benny and I were last. The sounds of the city above fell away, and a muffled silence settled in.

"I hope she's not an evil ghost who's leading us to our doom," Benny said. His voice echoed off the stone walls.

We walked further into the depths. Drips of water pinged off the floor of the tunnel, the sound reverberating in the darkness.

In addition to Mike's cell phone light, Duncan had also turned his on, but it didn't help us see anything but a few feet in front of us.

The ghost led us forward, stopping occasionally to make sure we were following.

I came to a halt. "Shhh." I cupped my hand to my ear. "Do you hear that?"

My friends paused to listen.

"What?" Cassandra whispered.

"The sound changed. Like when you go from a tight space to an open space."

April caught up with our ghost and motioned for us to follow. "Yeah! The tunnel is wider down here. There's a... a door."

"A door?" Cassandra scooted next to her friend and put her hand on the door knob. "Should we open it?"

The ghost looked directly at me and nodded. She turned toward the door and moved right through it.

We stared at each other in wide-eyed wonder.

"Did you see that?" April sputtered. "She went right through that door!"

I swallowed the lump in my throat. "What should we do?"

Cassandra squared her shoulders, steeling herself for an unseen battle. "Let's do this."

Slowly, she turned the knob and opened the door to a darkness so complete, my insides turned to jelly. As it creaked open, we huddled together, afraid to be separated from the safety of our pack. Slowly, we moved into the blackness that enveloped the space within.

"Turn on your cell phone flashlights," Mike whispered.

My hands shook as I pulled mine out of my pocket and flicked the app on.

"What the?" Benny gasped.

The walls of the cold, stone room glowed eerily in the light of our cell phones.

"My God," Duncan whispered.

The room was packed wall-to-wall with coffins.

## Chapter 21

"Holy…" April shrank back from the sight.

"What is this?" Cassandra whispered.

The ghost reappeared. She glided toward April, whose back was pressed against the wall near the doorway. April's face did not betray her fear, but her hands shook as she held them out in front of her as if in defense. "What do you want from me?"

I didn't sense any malice from the ghost. She had a mission, but I didn't think she meant to harm us in any way. "It's okay. She won't hurt you."

The ghost reached for April's bracelet—the one which had been passed down to her through generations. The women's long skirt rustled gently as she wrapped her ghostly fingers around the bracelet and April's wrist and then laid her other hand over her own heart.

"What is she saying?" April quivered and tried to pull her hand away from the specter's magnetic energy.

I finally understood. "She's trying to tell you that she's your ancestor. Your bracelet belonged to her long ago."

The ghost turned to me and nodded.

April gasped. "My ancestor?"

"What's your name?" I asked.

She mouthed something, but no sound came out. Had the rope that killed her severed her vocal cords? Before I had time to ask, she showed me an image of a red rose. It appeared in front of me like a shining hologram.

"Your name is Rose?" I asked.

She nodded.

"How did you know that?" Mike put his hand on my shoulder. "Did she say something that only you could hear?"

"No, but she showed me a rose. You didn't see it?" I looked up at him.

He shook his head. "No."

Rose floated past April through the doorway. April shivered and watched her ancestor disappear.

"Where is she going?" Benny asked. "And who are the people in those caskets?"

"I don't know, but she obviously wants us to follow her again." Cassandra charged ahead, and we crowded behind her as she trailed behind the ghostly woman.

Rose was already fifty or more yards ahead.

A shuffling sound echoed through the long tunnel.

"What is that?" I clutched Mike's arm.

A rat the size of terrier scuttled out from the shadows and ran over my foot.

I let out a long, piercing shriek. "Oh, my God!" My skin crawled. What was the phrase my mom always said? Heebie-jeebies. That was the perfect way to describe the creepy feeling I got during rat encounters. They gave me the heebee-jeebies.

Benny shivered and made a face. "I hate rats."

Duncan had caught up to Cassandra and pointed to Rose, who'd just disappeared through the wall. "There's another door."

"More coffins?" Mike hurried to see what Duncan was pointing to.

144

"I hope not." April turned the knob. The door creaked open. Rusty flecks of metal chipped away from the hinges and rained down on her outstretched arm. She shook the orange dust off and pushed the door inward. "Ready?"

We held our phone flashlights out and squeezed through the opening.

"OMG." Cassandra's face drained of color in the weak light.

My stomach dropped, and a queasy feeling bloomed inside me.

The stark white light from our many cell phones illuminated the space. The dirt, walls, and the floor of the vault seemed to be a rusty orange color. Shards of long stick-like limbs were piled on top of one another. Rib cages, metatarsals, and skulls. The bones all took on the same rusty hue.

My stomach dropped for the second time in the last few minutes.

Mike's face paled. He pulled his phone closer to his body. "I'm calling the police."

"There's no signal." Duncan had been one step ahead of Mike. "I've already tried."

I couldn't take my eyes off the bones piled haphazardly everywhere. My vision began to blur and suddenly, I felt myself slipping to the ground.

*Flash.*

*"But don't you think her family should know?"*

*"What for? She's just a servant girl. Her family was probably happy to get rid of her. Just another mouth to feed," the man's gruff voice said.*

*"What about this one?" A younger male stood holding the handles of a large wheelbarrow.*

*"Who cares? Just throw 'em in the cart. We don't have time or room to bury all of them. It'll be dark soon. We've got to move on."*

*Like a time-lapse film, I watched the comings and goings of people walking in and out of Washington Square Park. The women wore long skirts or dresses, with fancy hats perched on their heads. The men wore high-waisted trousers or suits with the chains of pocket watches dangling from their vests. Some were more casual and wore dirty clothes meant for hard labor.*

*I watched as two men cut the rope securing a woman to the branch of the hanging tree. The cart was underneath her and she fell into the cart with a sickening thud.*

*"What did this one do?" a man asked.*

*"I dunno. Something about a fire at the Lowell Estate. There wasn't much damage—just two or three stairs. Kitchen fire, I think it was."*

*"So, she started it?"*

*The man shrugged. "Maybe. They had to have someone to blame, so who knows?"*

*When the younger male rolled her body over, I recognized the ashen complexion and the long gray skirt. Angry red welts on her neck had turned a deep purple on the decaying flesh.*

*"Where do I take her?"*

*The older man pointed. "Down into the tunnel. There's a vault next to the one that belongs to the church's coffin-hold."*

*The young man wheeled the cart away, and soon Rose's body was no longer visible as he trundled the cart down into the tunnel.*


Someone was tapping my cheek with their palm. My eyes fluttered open.

"Jenny?" Mike hovered over me, his eyes full of concern. "Are you all right?"

He helped me sit up. I blinked at my friends and let my head clear for a moment before I could speak.

"Rose's body is in this room."

April put her hand over her mouth. "Oh, no. No wonder she led us down here. She wants to be put to rest."

I got to my feet. "Yes. She probably wants her remains to be identified. It would be great if the city could give her, and all of these people, a proper burial." My attention was drawn back to the pile of bones.

"This is like *CSI* or *Bones*." Cassandra's eyes sparkled with excitement. "The forensic scientists can come in and organize all the bones and identify them through dental records or something."

"Dental records?" Benny said. "I'm sure most of the people they shoved down here were too poor to afford a dentist. Otherwise, they would've been buried in a cemetery. Sorry to say, I don't think they can identify any of these bodies."

Cassandra pooched her lower lip out. "That's not right. Poor people should be given the same kind of dignity in death as anyone else."

"I agree." April glanced at the piles of bones. "But that's the way it was back then. And in some cases, that's the way it is today. Not much has changed."

My eyes drifted back to the human remains. A haze of light-colored dust arose from the pile. "What is that?" I stepped toward the skeletons.

"What is what?" Duncan asked.

"Do you see the haze there?" I pointed to the bones.

Everyone but Benny shook their heads. "I see it." Benny craned his neck. "There's more in that corner."

Slowly, the hazy forms came together, until there were several people in transparent form standing in the shadows. Rose, in solid form, pointed toward the people.

There was a small man who looked to be of Italian descent clutching a rosary. He was wearing a dusty white shirt and trousers with suspenders. His eyes pleaded with me. What did he want? Why hadn't he crossed over after he'd passed away?

"What happened to you?" I asked him.

*"I don't know."* His eyes were encircled with dark red rings, like he hadn't slept in years. I supposed that was accurate, given the time period he'd died in.

Relieved that he was able to speak, I asked. "Do you remember the last thing you were doing before you found yourself here?"

My friends exchanged glances, looking confused. But Benny was focused on the man, as I was.

I whispered to them, "It's one of the people here. He doesn't know the circumstances of his death."

*"My death?"* The man's eyebrows shot up. *"I'm not dead. I woke up here. Where am I?"*

"You're in the subway tunnels. But, I'm very sorry to say, that yes, you are dead."

He narrowed his eyes. *"No. That can't be."* He had a strong Italian accent. *"I just found a job—a good one, too. I am saving money to bring my wife and children here from the old country."*

"Sir, I'm so sorry. Have you been sick recently?" I needed to find a reason for him. He had to know what'd killed him, so he could accept it and move on.

He frowned and looked down at the rosary in his hand. *"I was not feeling very well. The flu, I think. Why am I holding onto my mother's rosary? I don't remember…"*

"There were lots of people dying from the flu and other illnesses in the 1800s," Benny said. "It could've been any number of those."

*"Why do you keep saying I am dead? I need to get to my new job. How do I find my way out of here? Can you help me?"*

My heart broke for him. "Can you tell me what year it is?"

He glowered at me like I was a crazy person. *"Don't you know? It's 1805, of course."*

148

I shook my head. "That was a very long time ago. Over two hundred years have passed since then. It's now 2019."

His eyes widened. *"You're crazy!"* But then he took a hard look at my friends, his eyes inspecting our clothing and hairstyles—and our cell phone flashlights. *"Mio Dio."*

"What's going on?" Cassandra was clearly not happy that she didn't know what was going on. She couldn't see the man or hear his end of the conversation.

Remembering what Isla had told me, I reached out and grabbed Cassandra's hand. Her eyes grew wide. "I can see him," she said.

"Yellow fever was an epidemic back then. It could've killed him," Duncan said.

"Possibly. But whatever it was, it took his life, and he didn't even realize it." I turned my attention back to the man. "What is your name?"

*"Vincenzo Barone."*

"Vincenzo." I held my arms up. "Do you see a light anywhere?"

He pointed at our cell phones. *"Many lights coming from those little things you are holding."*

"No," I continued. "I mean, do you see a light somewhere else? Maybe in the distance?"

He looked around and wrinkled his forehead. *"Yes. There is something bright over there."* He pointed vaguely in the direction behind me.

"If you go toward the light, I think you'll see your wife. And your children. They've been waiting for you."

He raised his eyebrows. *"They are here? In this place?"*

"They have crossed over to a beautiful place where you can all be together. They've been waiting for you for a long, long time."

He didn't look convinced. But, he started in the direction he'd pointed to earlier. *"Ah! I cannot believe it. I see them. My darling, Camila, and my bambinos, too!"*

149

"Good, Vincenzo!" I smiled as he rushed past me. "Go to them. They'll help you get to where you need to go."

He turned to look over his shoulder. *"Thank you for helping me. You are very kind."*

I watched him walk until he disappeared into a light that scattered dust particles like snowflakes. "He made it."

Benny sighed. "You're good. But what about all the others?" He pointed to the bones.

Glancing at the pile of remains, I saw the misty shapes of people emerging in the gloom. They, too, looked frightened and confused. "It's all right," I told them. "Follow Vincenzo." I pointed toward the place where he'd gone. "Your families are there, waiting for you."

A little boy wearing short pants and a cap was the first one to run to the light. He didn't even look back—it was as if he'd been just waiting for someone to give him permission to go.

As soon as he vanished into the light, the others smiled. They glided after him and disappeared into a burst of brightness.

The shining light dimmed, leaving only the illumination coming from our cell phones.

"What about Rose?" April asked. "Did she cross over? I didn't get a chance to say goodbye."

I shook my head. "I didn't see her. Benny, did you?"

"No. But maybe she went with everyone else and we didn't notice."

Mike opened the door as wide it as it could go. "We need to get out of here and call the police."

# Chapter 22

Once we got to street level, it was late. The flow of traffic had lessened, and a light rain had made the surfaces of the roads shiny and dark.

Mike reached for his phone to call the police.

"No," I said. "Let me do that. I have a connection there."

He raised his eyebrows but didn't protest.

I made the call and listened while the phone rang on the other end. A few seconds went by and then Detective Caruso's voice said, "Jenny? Is everything okay?"

"Sort of, I guess." I glanced at my friends, who were shifting their weight from one foot to the other, trying to keep warm. The contrast between the temperature in the subway and the street level was jarring.

"What's wrong?" His voice carried a hint of concern.

"My friends and I discovered a bunch of bodies." It wasn't a brilliant way to put it, but I couldn't think of anything clever.

"Wait a minute. Did you say bodies?"

"Unfortunately, yes. Lots of bones in the subway."

"Jesus," he murmured. "Give me the location. I'll send out medical examiners, ambulances, and get my team out there."

I listened to the sound of a siren wailing in the distance, wondering what other crisis the police were headed to on this dark night. "No need for ambulances, Detective. These people have been dead a long, long time. We found them in an abandoned subway tunnel."

There was a long pause. "I'm afraid to ask why you were in a section of an abandoned subway tunnel. Why don't you just tell me where you are?"

I gave him the street names and ended the call. "The police will be here soon."

We huddled together on the sidewalk and watched the cars go by.

"So much for a fun get-together in NYC," Benny said wryly.

"Oh, come on." Cassandra grinned. "It was an adventure and you know it. Thousands of tourists come here each year. But ten years from now, how much will they remember about their trip?"

Benny shrugged.

"That's right. They won't remember much. But we, on the other hand, will remember this forever. How many people can say they crept down an abandoned subway tunnel and discovered not one, but two rooms full of human remains?" Cassandra put her hand on her hip. "And don't forget, we got to interact with ghosts. It was freakin' awesome!"

Benny laughed. "I suppose that's true. I will never forget being led under the streets of New York City by a ghost who pointed us toward piles of dead bodies."

"My first trip to the States has been a truly memorable occasion," Duncan said. "Wait until I tell my uncle about this. He'll probably want to be on the next flight to see what else we can discover."

"Good old Professor Greenbough." Benny winked. "He'd go straight down that tunnel, and we'd probably never see him again. He'd want to explore every part of the subway system, hoping to find more bones and ghosts."

Sirens blared in the night air.

I pulled my light jacket tighter around me. "The police are here."

An unmarked vehicle came barreling around the corner and stopped in front of us. Behind it came police cars with blue and red lights spinning.

A curious late-night dog walker craned her neck, trying to see what all the fuss was about. Her two dogs shied away from the commotion and pulled her in the opposite direction.

Detective Caruso got out of the first unmarked vehicle and approached us. "Hi, kids. Tell me what's going on."

Everyone started talking at one time. The detective put out his hand to stop us. "Slow down. How about just one of you tells me what happened?"

As other police officers arrived, I got a little nervous. There was no way I was going to tell them about Rose leading us to the bodies. "We were coming back from a night out when we noticed the construction on this corner," I said. "I saw an opening below. Once I stepped on that concrete block down there, I spotted a heavy board leaning against the dirt wall."

"And?" the detective asked.

I gave him a sheepish grin. "I was curious and pushed it aside. That's when I realized there was a tunnel down there."

He shook his head. "So, you decided to explore."

The other police officers' eyes narrowed. I could tell they were suspicious of my story.

"Yeah. We thought it would be cool to see what's down there."

"That was stupid." Detective Caruso frowned.

"It was my fault." April stepped forward. "It was my idea to go down there, not Jenny's."

"No, it was my idea." Cassandra stuck her chin out. "I saw a documentary about old, abandoned subway tunnels and didn't want to miss an opportunity to see it for myself."

Detective Caruso rolled his eyes. "Okay, okay. I get it. You were all at fault. Fine. You know, you could be arrested for trespassing, right?" His lip twitched when he saw our stricken faces. He groaned. "Show me what you found."

When we headed for the opening in the ground, the detective said, "Jenny, you lead the way." He turned to my friends. "You guys stay up here. Officer Mahoney will take your statements. Officers Santos and Briggs will come with us down into the tunnel."

I looked over my shoulder at my friends, who mostly looked sad they weren't going under the street with us. I suspected it was because it was a lot warmer below than it was up here.

Just before I turned my attention back to Detective Caruso, I noticed some motion across the street. Braydon Dudek clumsily slipped behind a tree, its trunk barely concealing the hulk of his large body. I was beginning to think he'd read too many *Harriet the Spy* books as a child. Why was he always lurking around every corner?

"This way." I stepped down into the underground entrance.

The detective and officers followed, grumbling as they stooped to avoid hitting their heads. Once they turned on their flashlights, the corridor was illuminated.

I went ahead to show them the way to the first door. Pushing it open with a creak, I pointed to the coffins inside.

Officer Santos gasped. She turned her gaze on me. "Caskets?"

"Maybe they're empty." Officer Briggs, a big man, put on gloves and stepped forward to inspect the coffin nearest us. His body blocked the light from Officer Santos' flashlight, and she stepped around him to shine the light from a different angle.

154

I chewed on my lip. I knew the coffins weren't empty. I could feel it.

Briggs unlatched the clasps on the plain wooden casket. Dust erupted from the lid as he wrenched it open.

As the light from Caruso's and Santos' flashlights hit the contents inside, Officer Briggs groaned. "Oh, God."

I peeked into the coffin. The white bones glinted in the rays of light. I stifled a scream. There wasn't just one skeleton inside—there were two. One tiny one folded in half, inside the larger skeleton.

"She died in childbirth." Detective Caruso's face was solemn. "The baby looks breach."

Santos sighed. "So, so sad. The bodies have been here a long time. I wonder if they're all this old."

"I'll call a forensic team when we get back on top. Let's tape this room off when we leave." Caruso went through the door. "Let's go."

"Wait!" I held my hand up. "There's another room with more bodies. But they aren't in coffins."

Briggs turned to me, one eyebrow raised. "How long were you kids down here?"

"Not too long. We just went a little way down the tunnel and found another door."

"Show us," Caruso said.

\*\*\*

Twenty minutes later, we were back on the street. The police were still surrounding the area, but had finished interviewing my friends. They'd gone into full shiver mode as the night temperature dropped even lower.

"Can you believe that?" Cassandra shook her head. "We found bodies. Bodies! Under the street. God, I love New York City."

Benny laughed. "That's what I like about you, Cassandra. You find the good in everything."

"You have to admit." Duncan grinned. "Cassandra's not wrong. Finding bodies will be the highlight of my inaugural voyage to America."

"Definitely something to text home about." I wanted to laugh, but the thought of all those forgotten people tossed in a pile, rotting away for two hundred years, made me sad.

"It's super late." Cassandra hugged herself. "You guys want to rush a Broadway show in the morning? You can only get last-minute tickets for the hot shows if you get there super early. Like pre-dawn."

"Sure," I said. "And if we can't all get tickets together, we can enter the ticket lottery and break up into twos. We're bound to win a couple of them."

"What's a ticket lottery?" Benny asked.

"You can get Broadway tickets in the lottery for only ten bucks." Cassandra flicked a curl off her cheek. "Perfect way to see a show when you're a poor college student."

"Then we'd better head back to the hotel if we're going to get up early." Benny yawned. "I'm pretty tired from traveling and college visits. Plus, discovering bodies is exhausting."

I glanced longingly at Mike and wished we'd had an opportunity for alone time. "Hang on for a second." I pulled Mike away from the group. "Can we have a date tomorrow? Just the two of us?"

"I'd like that." He leaned down and kissed me gently on the lips. "We'll make plans after our early morning wait in line."

\*\*\*

When Cassandra and I got back to our room, we collapsed onto our beds.

"What a night." She arranged the pillows behind her head and sighed. "The whole ghost thing is taking me right back to our trip to Europe this summer. So many ghosts…"

156

"Yeah, I know." I took off my jacket and slung it onto the chair next to my bed. "I thought we were done with ghosts."

Cassandra giggled. "Jenny, you will never be done with ghosts. They can see you coming a mile away—and they all want you to solve their problems."

"You're not wrong." I sighed. "Do you think Rose crossed over? I'm hoping she got enough closure for her to have some peace."

Cassandra shrugged. "I don't know. You said you didn't see her cross over with the others."

I thought back to the dark tunnel. I'd watched Vincenzo and his fellow ghost-mates walk into the light, but I didn't remember seeing Rose go with them.

"I didn't see her go," I said. "But I hope she made it."

"Me too." Cassandra got up and quickly dressed in her pajamas. She scrabbled under the covers and pulled them up to her chin. "I'm so tired. We have to rest up for tomorrow. We're going to spend the day on the town."

I hesitated. "About that. I'm hoping to have a date with just Mike tomorrow. But I don't want to ignore Benny. I mean, he came all the way from Seattle…"

Cassandra rolled over to face me. "How about we spend time with him part of the day, have alone time with our boyfriends, then meet up for a show at night?"

I thought for a moment. "Yeah, I guess that works. I'll run it by Mike in the morning, but it sounds like a good plan to me."

Cassandra's eyelids drooped. "Good." She yawned and tugged the blanket under her chin.

"Go to sleep." I smiled at her, but her eyes were already closed.

"That's exactly how I feel." I got ready for bed and sank into sleep almost immediately.

157

*Charity had eluded me long enough. It was time for me to bring her home to the marriage bed. Hope and Faith had waited patiently, and so had I.*

*Outside the all-night city grocery store, I waited for her to come out. She'd been in there for at least fifteen minutes.*

*I could almost taste victory as she finally stepped out onto the sidewalk.*

*My heart pounded as I surveilled the area. Were there witnesses close enough to catch a glimpse of me?*

*Carefully, I crept out from behind the dumpster I was hiding behind.*

*Oh, she was so perfect. Brains, beauty, healing powers. She had it all.*

*I licked my dry lips. Just a few more steps and I'd have her for my very own.*

*The bag of groceries she was carrying would surely be to my advantage. With only one hand to defend herself, she would be an easy conquest.*

*"Charity," I whispered.*

*Her head snapped to attention. Did she see me?*

*A large armored van rumbled toward us. I had to get to her before it was too late!*

*The cross light turned green and the van accelerated. No!*

*I scrambled to the curb, waiting for the vehicle to pass. When it rolled by in a cloud of exhaust, I blinked. She was gone.*

Once again, I woke up shaking. It was just a matter of time before this man got his prize. What was his plan for the three women?

Shivering, I pulled a hoodie over my head and tugged it down. What time was it? My cell said it was 3:00 a.m. My fingers hovered over the screen. Should I call Detective Caruso?

"No," I whispered. I couldn't do that to him. What could he follow up on? The man didn't get the woman named Charity. Not this time. How could I keep him from taking her?

Deep down, I knew what I had to do. I had to find out who the man was and where he lived. More importantly, I had to find the women he'd already taken and get them to safety.

I laid back down in bed and stared at the ceiling. If I had to have a sleepless night, it should be because I was thinking about something good, like Mike. Instead, thoughts of the scary man slithered through my brain like worms. The police had nothing to go on. They didn't even know the women were missing. Only I knew. And I had to figure out a way to find them.

## Chapter 23

Though it was still dark outside, the city was awake. Bags of trash were sitting alongside the sidewalk awaiting garbage pick-up. Busy folks were dutifully marching past us as they made their way to their destinations. The line to get tickets was long and wrapped around the corner of the street. I was thankful we'd gotten here early.

"Why did we agree to do this?" April rubbed her eyes. "The sun isn't even up yet."

"Because we want tickets to see *Dear Evan Hansen* tonight." Cassandra said.

"And why do we want to see this overpriced show?" April scowled. "I'm not really into musicals."

Benny gaped at her. "I mean, I hear ya on the 'it's too early' thing. But come on. Everybody is raving about this show. I can't leave New York City without seeing it."

April grumbled under her breath.

Benny shoved his Starbucks into her hands. "Here. Drink this. You'll feel better."

My mouth dropped open. "You're giving her your coffee? The man who cannot live without his coffee is giving it away?"

He made a face. "I'm not *giving* it to her. I'm letting her have a few sips. Then I'm taking it back."

"That sounds more like the Benny I know." I laughed.

"Look! They've opened the box office." Duncan pointed.

"Oh, good." I shuffled forward with the rest of our group. "We're fifth in line, so I think we'll get them."

I was right. Thankfully, we managed to snap up tickets—though we weren't all sitting together. We got groups of twos scattered in the orchestra level.

"These are great seats," Mike said.

"Benny, is it okay if you and April sit together? The rest of us are couples."

"Rub it in, why don't you?" Benny sighed. "I wish Caleb was here."

"But then I wouldn't have anyone to sit with." April nudged him playfully.

He grinned. "You've got a point."

"How is Caleb, anyway?" I asked. Benny and Caleb had started dating after our trip to Europe. It was clear to me that they made the perfect couple. Caleb was an artsy theatre guy. Benny was a detail-oriented master of technology, but he also had a creative side to him, especially when it came to film. He'd been working on a number of projects after we'd come home from Europe. He'd make a great director or producer someday.

"He's great," Benny said. "He's visiting colleges now too. He applied to some of the universities I have. It would be awesome if we ended up attending the same one."

I looked at Mike. "Yeah, that would be nice. I wish we would've ended up in the same school."

He nodded. "But this is okay. I'm only a few hours away."

"True. And maybe we'd get on each other's nerves if we were at the same school and in the same program." I leaned into him.

161

Mike laughed. "You might get sick of me, but I'd never get sick of you."

I stood on my tiptoes and kissed his cheek. "You're sweet."

Once we had our tickets, Cassandra and Duncan went off to visit the Empire State Building. Benny and April decided to check out the Metropolitan Museum of Art. Mike and I decided to get breakfast and take a walk in Central Park.

The sun had risen, kissing the tops of buildings and icing our hair with a rosy light. I held Mike's hand as we watched a young couple climb into a horse-drawn carriage and clop down a narrow, paved road in the park.

A bicyclist whizzed past us.

"Let's walk along the lake," Mike said.

We turned toward a little cut-off path and walked along the water. Everything was so beautiful, even the black, rod-iron fencing that separated us from the lake.

"Thanks for coming to visit." I grinned up at him.

"Why are you thanking me?" He asked. "Spending time with you means a lot."

A duck took off from the water's surface and joined a group of his friends on the gravel bank.

"I guess it's time we meet up with everyone." I squeezed his hand, savoring the remaining minutes of our time alone before heading back.

\*\*\*

We were lucky to find a small table at the upscale coffeehouse near the park. The scent of fresh baked pastries and perfectly brewed coffee filled the air.

I'd just finished telling him the entire story of the guy who seemed to be collecting women and stowing them away in a dungeon-like environment.

I took a sip of my expensive latte, enjoying the creamy foam on top. "So, what should I do?"

He took a bite of his apple fritter and chewed thoughtfully. "Honestly, I don't know. You said the police don't have reports of any missing women that fit the descriptions you gave?"

My shoulders slumped. "No. But why aren't they being reported missing? Wouldn't their families or friends notice they were gone?"

"Unless they were supposed to be gone anyway?" He raised his eyebrows.

"Huh?"

"What if the women said they were going on vacation or something? Then their families wouldn't be worried if they hadn't heard from them."

"I hadn't thought of that." I munched my chocolate croissant. "I suppose that's a possibility. But it seems like way too much of a coincidence to capture women who were planning a vacation."

Mike set his coffee down. "What if the guy did it?"

"Did what?"

"Texted the families. He could've taken their phones and sent texts to their friends, co-workers, bosses…"

"Telling them they were going on a spontaneous vacation. That's brilliant!" I smiled at him. "You're pretty smart, you know that?"

"Not as smart as you." He leaned forward and gave me a quick kiss on the lips.

My smile faded as I realized that if Mike's theory was correct, it would take much, much longer for the families to know something was wrong. I remembered I'd planned to call the police, but with all the excitement of getting up early and waiting in line, I'd neglected to call. "I need to phone Detective Caruso. Maybe he can do something."

"Let's enjoy breakfast first." Mike reached across the table and squeezed my hand. "Then call him before we meet up with the rest of the group."

\*\*\*

The detective didn't have much to offer in the way of ideas. "You don't have any details I can use yet. But if you have more visions, let me know. By the way, I went to the hospital early this morning and found an employee there named Dr. Charity Nelson. She's an obstetrician. Dr. Nelson was there on-call during the night. When I asked her if someone had been following her, she had a bit of a breakdown."

"She did?"

"Yeah. I got her a cup of tea to let her pull herself together before I asked her for an explanation."

"I feel so bad for her. The visions I had were scary— he's almost captured her two or three times."

"That's what she told me. Last night, she went to the all-night grocer during her break, and she swears she saw a guy staring at her from across the street."

My heart thumped with excitement. "That's what I saw in my dream. Can she describe the man? I still don't know what he looks like."

"Unfortunately, no. She said he was wearing all black. But she did say his skin was pale. So at least we know he's Caucasian."

I closed my eyes, wishing I'd been able to see more in the visions. "Well, that narrows it down."

He chuckled. "Right."

"Will the police keep her safe? I hope you have someone protecting her at all times." I bit my lip, worried that it was just a matter of time before the man took her.

"Yes. Now that she's confirmed someone is stalking her, we've assigned protection."

I breathed out a sigh of relief. "Thank you."

"Okay, if you get anything else, call me right away."

"Wait!" I said. "What about the coffins and bones we found last night?"

"I'm on my way back to the site right now. Our forensic team said those bodies have been down there since the 1800s."

"What are you going to do with the remains? Surely, there aren't any family members you can contact."

"No," he said. "We need to confer with the city to see if there is precedent. If this issue has come up before, we need to know how it was handled."

It was clear he had many hours of work ahead of him. "Good luck, Detective."

## Chapter 24

The evening was dry but chilly. New York City was buzzing with activity, as usual. We stood outside in a crowd, eager to see *Dear Evan Hansen*. I moved closer to Mike as more patrons pushed the line forward.

"This day was perfect." I looped my arm through Mike's.

"It was one of the best days ever."

Cassandra grinned as she looked up at Duncan. "My feet are tired after exploring the city. We must've covered everything within a ten-mile radius."

Duncan kissed her nose. "But we can rest while we watch the show."

"I met up with Frank after April and I left the museum," Benny said.

"I miss Frank!" I was very fond of the old guy. I hadn't seen him since we returned from our European trip. "I hope we see him before you leave."

"Why don't you meet us for breakfast tomorrow morning?" Benny asked. "We're visiting another school in the early afternoon. We fly back to Seattle in the evening."

"Sounds good. Text me when you get up."

The line moved faster, and soon we were inside the theatre and scattered off to find our seats.

Mike and I had seats on the left side of the orchestra level, with a good view of the stage.

When the curtain rose, I was transported back to high school. I empathized with the main character's sense of isolation and feelings of abandonment. In my junior year, I'd finally admitted to myself I had a gift. It hadn't been easy. My friends had turned their backs on me for a while, and it had been rough.

Finally, the first act ended, and the house lights went up. I turned to Mike and squeezed his hand. "That was intense, but really good."

"For sure. I'd love to be cast in this show someday." He got up and stretched.

"Me too. Want to go meet the others in the lobby?"

"Sure."

We found Benny and April in the line for refreshments.

"Where's Cassandra and Duncan?" I peered into the sea of people heading out of the auditorium.

"There they are." April pointed to the back of the lobby. They were stealing a kiss near the water fountain.

"So cute, those two." I smiled. "It's nice that Duncan could surprise her."

"They are sickeningly adorable together." Benny sighed. "But it's good to see them so happy."

We each bought a cookie and quickly munched them down.

"Think there's time to go to the bathroom?" April asked as the lights flashed for the five-minute warning.

"Probably. If we hurry."

Mike and Benny waited while April and I scurried to the women's restroom.

The bathroom's cloying, artificial orange scent made me wrinkle my nose. I washed my hands quickly as the lights blinked again. It was the two-minute warning. We needed to get back to our seats.

The blinking lights made my head spin. Dizziness crept up on me as I dried my hands with a paper towel. I grabbed for the sink to steady myself.

*Flash.*

*Charity was heading into room 301. The patient in that room had just been admitted at the beginning of her labor. The police officer assigned to protect her was standing right outside the room.*

*The scent of antiseptics and cleaners filled my nose. I inhaled deeply. Healers were of the Divine. God had put me here to collect my darling wife. He had put me here to serve.*

*Now was my chance to take her.*

*I looked down at the scrubs I'd grabbed from a supply closet minutes before. They were a little snug, but they worked. A stethoscope I'd snatched from the counter in the break room hung around my neck. I smiled as I realized the Lord always provided for true believers.*

*Now if I could only get rid of the cop.*

*I scooted toward the red fire alarm near one of the exits. A group of people bustled by. This was it. I pulled the alarm.*

*The siren wailed, and the corridor lights flashed.*

*The officer stiffened and moved closer to my treasure.*

*"Excuse me!" I ran to him. "I saw a man with a gun!"*

*He drew his weapon and pushed Charity behind him. "Where?"*

*I pointed toward the far end of the hall. "He just went into room 320."*

*"Stay right here with him," the officer told Charity. He ran against the tide of people rushing to get out of the building.*

*"Don't worry." I smiled at my beauty. "You're safe with me."*

"Jenny!"

168

I felt someone's fingers tapping my cheek. Awareness settled back into my body. The orange-scented air freshener made my nose twitch. My eyes fluttered open.

April hovered over me. "Are you all right?"

April helped me up from the floor. "Did you have a vision?"

My stomach dropped. "Yeah. He's got her. I've got to call Detective Caruso."

\*\*\*

There was nothing I could do after I'd called Detective Caruso. He'd taken the information and promised to call me when he knew more.

Between songs, I snuck back to my seat next to Mike.

He reached over and grabbed my hand. "Is everything all right?" he whispered.

"No. It's not. I'll tell you after the show." I squeezed his hand tighter.

My stomach churned during the second act. Thoughts of Charity haunted me. What would the man do to her? I knew in my gut it was nothing good.

Mike and I kept exchanging worried glances. I knew he was feeling anxious that he couldn't help.

The music from the show helped calm me a little, but I couldn't follow the storyline anymore.

When the show was over, I didn't remember how it had ended.

# Chapter 25

Cassandra and I hurried to get ready. We were meeting everyone for breakfast. Except April—she had to work on a project for her digital art class.

My eyes burned from lack of sleep. Detective Caruso hadn't called me back after I'd talked to him the night before. I knew it was a bad sign. If he'd been able to find Charity and arrest her kidnapper, he would've called me.

Cassandra yanked the door open. "Let's go. I hope we're not too late."

I ran to catch up with her as she flew down the stairs and out the front door of the building.

"Why are you in such a hurry?" I huffed. "We still have ten minutes until we have to be there."

She frowned. "Frank is always early. Once a military guy, always a military guy. Their whole lives are synchronized to the correct time."

I shrugged and jogged after her. "I guess."

The sun was out, but the air carried the impending chill of autumn. A taxi honked at a pedestrian who was too slow getting across the street.

Stopping at the crosswalk, she turned to me. "I guess I'm excited to see Frank. I miss the old guy."

"Me too." I ran after her as she scurried across the road.

When we arrived at our favorite coffee shop a few blocks from Washington Square Park, the scent of java and cinnamon made my stomach growl.

Frank, Benny, Duncan, and Mike were already there. We hugged Frank, ordered our coffee and food, and settled into our seats. I glanced at Benny and did a double-take. There were dark circles under his eyes.

"Did you stay up all night?" I joked.

He glared at Frank. "It's not that. *Someone* made us get here a half hour early."

Frank snickered. "You kids have it too easy these days. When I was a youngster, I had to get up at four o'clock every morning to start my newspaper route. I finished at seven, then ate breakfast and went to school."

"I bet you had to walk uphill both ways... in the snow," Benny grumbled.

Frank grinned. "Yup."

I couldn't help but notice that the older man was looking spry and happy. Having Benny living with him was doing him some good. And the fact that he'd reunited with his daughters and his grandchildren was definitely having a positive impact on his life. He was no longer a lonely old man.

"What have you been up to, Frank?" I sipped my coffee.

"Oh, not much, except for going on this trip, of course. And I got to meet up with some of my old army buddies. We tried to keep out of trouble, but you know what they say..."

"What do they say?" Cassandra chirped.

"Few things are harder to put up with than a good example."

Cassandra frowned. "What does that mean?"

"It means that we weren't good examples." Frank chuckled.

One side of Benny's mouth quirked up. "I don't want to know."

"Then I won't tell you." Frank chucked Benny's arm lightly. "I don't want to give you any ideas."

Cassandra leaned over and whispered to Benny, "I don't get it."

"It's okay," he said under his breath. "It's old man humor. Only old men get it."

"So," Mike said, "you're flying back to Seattle later tonight?"

"Yeah." Benny frowned. "I don't really want to go back. I like this city."

"I hope you get admitted to one of the schools here," I said. "We could see each other on a regular basis."

Duncan looked down at his cinnamon roll. "You guys are making me wish I lived here. I love my university mates, but you guys get into the most interesting paranormal situations. And you're fun too."

"What if you transferred?" Mike asked.

Duncan ran his fingers through his tousled, sandy-colored hair. "I don't know. I'm already beginning my third year at Oxford. It might be odd to switch schools more than halfway through. And all of my credits may not be transferrable. I don't want to risk it."

Cassandra sighed. "True. But maybe you can look into it."

He nodded. "I can. But in the meantime, I'm happy to come over to the States to visit."

"Yes!" She clapped her hands. "You must visit lots and lots of times."

Frank, clearly tired of our chattering, cleared his throat. "So, what's this I hear about your latest visions, Jenny?"

I put down the scone I'd been munching. "Benny probably told you. There's a man who's been kidnapping women. For some strange reason, he's obsessed with creating the perfect wife. It seems like a religious thing—

something about the trinity. Three women—and he's shackled them."

Frank's brows drew together, and his eyes darkened. "What a sick bastard. Do you know who he is?"

"Not yet. But I'm really worried for those women."

"I'm concerned about you," Frank said. "It makes me nervous that you're handling this all alone. Wish I could stay and help."

I felt bad. I didn't want to drag everyone into this mess. Benny had more college visits to focus on. Frank had his family to dote on. "Don't worry. I'm working with the police. They'll keep me safe."

# Chapter 26

I stood on my tiptoes and kissed Mike. Warmth spread through me. I wanted to keep kissing him like this forever. But, the bus back to Ithaca was leaving in just a few minutes.

He held me tight. "See you in a few weeks?"

We'd decided to take turns visiting each another for the rest of the school year. It was my turn to visit him next. I was excited to meet his friends and explore the little town he lived in.

"I can't wait." I hugged him tight.

Mike glanced at the Port Authority board displaying the bus departure time. "I've got to go." He cupped his hands around my face and gave me one more amazing kiss. "I love you."

"Love you too." I watched him walk toward the entryway to the passenger loading platform.

Suddenly, I felt alone and vulnerable. I watched the flow of people bustling around me, heading toward destinations unknown. I had to go back to campus on the subway. But which exit was the right one? I couldn't remember which door we'd come through.

My gaze paused on the figure of a broad man with a beard. Was that Braydon Dudek? Had he been following me?

An ember of fury ignited inside me. The slow burn of it rose from my chest into my throat. I wanted to scream. What kind of sick person was he? Why was he following me? I rushed after him, accidentally bumping into at least two people as I attempted to catch up.

Braydon disappeared through an exit.

I dashed after him and stopped abruptly when I emerged into the full daylight. New York City was alive with millions of people swarming the sidewalks, hurrying in and out of buildings, and walking purposefully across intersections.

Which way had he gone?

I walked one direction and couldn't spot him in the crowd. Turning a one-eighty, I rushed in the opposite direction, my eyes searching for his broad shape. He was nowhere to be found.

Had I imagined seeing him? Was it just someone who looked similar?

My phone buzzed in my pocket. The flames of anger burning inside me were doused when I saw the name and number flash on the screen. It was Detective Caruso.

"Jenny, I'd like to meet with you sometime soon. We need to know everything you can give us about the man who kidnapped the doctor at the hospital."

"I've told you everything I know. I'm not sure if I can help." I had given up running after Braydon, but I was still scanning the sidewalks, hoping to catch a glimpse of him.

He cleared his throat. "We're pretty good at questioning. Sometimes asking from a fresh perspective can jog memories you didn't even know you had."

I snapped out of my surliness and focused on the call. "You're right. When do you want to meet?"

"Can you be at the precinct in an hour?"

What the hell. Homework could wait another couple of hours. "Sure. I'll be there."

*** 

Since I had an hour to kill, I wandered through Times Square and then the theatre district. I bought a sandwich and a milkshake and found a place to eat on a concrete stoop.

Pigeons strutted past and eyed the tidbits I'd dropped on the sidewalk. I watched one make a daring move to capture one of the pieces. "Go ahead. I won't hurt you."

He gave me a suspicious look, but with one quick movement forward, snatched the crumb and retreated.

My thoughts wandered to Braydon. Had he really followed Mike and me to the bus station? Or was I imagining every stranger with a similar shape to be him? And if that was the case, why was I so paranoid?

I checked the time. I had a half hour to get to the precinct. Crumpling the sandwich wrapper into a ball, I threw it and the empty milkshake cup into the nearest garbage can.

After hopping on the subway and arriving at my destination, I took the elevator up to Detective Caruso's floor and checked in with the officer at the desk.

Caruso was waiting for me in his office. He stood up when I entered the room. "Hi, Jenny. Have a seat."

There were two seats on the opposite side of his desk. I picked the one closest to the wall.

"Thanks for coming in." He sat down and flipped open a page of his notebook, ignoring the laptop next to him. "Let's concentrate on the guy who kidnapped the woman from the hospital."

I swallowed hard. I knew he was looking for new information—something I hadn't told him already. "What would you like to know?"

"Everything you can think of. Let's start with the kidnapping. Tell me, in detail, what you experienced in your vision."

I replayed the scene in my head. "I was looking through his eyes. I was wearing blue scrubs. They fit a little too snug, but I was sure no one would notice."

He jotted something down in his notebook. "Good. What else?"

My thoughts drifted back to when the kidnapper was standing next to Charity and the police officer. What could I tell him that I hadn't already said?

"Maybe this will help," the detective said. "Let's start with the physical aspects of seeing through the eyes of the kidnapper. Where were you looking when you saw Charity and the officer? Were you looking up at either of them? Down?"

I was finally understanding what he was getting at. "Are you asking what height the kidnapper was in relation to the woman and the policeman?"

He nodded. "Exactly."

Thinking back, I realized that my eyes—or the kidnapper's eyes—were level with the officer. Charity's eyes were quite a bit lower. I sat up straighter. "The kidnapper is the same height as the cop. And he's about four or five inches taller than the woman."

"Excellent!" He gave me a broad smile. "I'll check with Officer Brady to get his height. I'll look up Charity's too. Now, let's go back to what you said about the scrubs fitting snugly. Were the pants too tight? Were they the right length or were they too short?"

I closed my eyes and tried to visualize. Had I looked down at my pantlegs? Yes. I had. The pants fit well in the length—not too short. Wait a minute. I opened my eyes. "The pants fit fine in the length. But the shoes were weird. No one else at the hospital was wearing anything similar."

"Good, good." Detective Caruso jotted down more notes. "Since the length was fine for the scrubs, it leads me to believe that the man is a bit overweight. Because if the pants weren't too short, the scrubs may have been tight because he was bigger around on the top."

My mind wandered back to the shoes. There was something familiar about them. Before I could say anything, the detective looked up from his notebook.

"Describe the shoes."

"Huh. Strange," I said.

"What?" He leaned forward.

"I think the shoes were navy blue Vans. I've never seen hospital personnel wearing Vans. Usually, they wear athletic shoes or those clunky clogs."

"Guess he should've given his disguise a little more thought. Thankfully he didn't—that's to our advantage." He jotted something down and then chewed on the end of his pencil. "This is helpful. Let's go over it again. Describe every single detail you can remember."

An hour and a half later, I left the precinct exhausted.

By the time I got back to school, it was early evening. I wandered into the cafeteria, dished up some mac 'n cheese and salad, and sat down to eat. Taking a sip of my water, I glanced around the expanse of the cafeteria.

My heart jumped as I spotted Braydon Dudek dumping his tray in the receptacle. Thank God he hadn't seen me. I sighed with relief.

I watched as he pushed the doors open. Just then, I noticed his feet. He was wearing faded, navy blue Vans.

My blood pounded in my ears. Oh my God! Without hesitation, I whipped out my phone and called the detective. I explained about the shoes and gave him Braydon's name.

"I'll have someone tail him," Detective Caruso said. "But I can't bring him in for questioning just because he's wearing the same brand of shoes. We have no probable cause to suspect him."

"But what about the scrubs? They were tight. Braydon is a big guy. It's one more thing that points to him."

"Again, if it's based on body type and shoes, I can't question people because of their size or the brand of shoes they wear if there's no other link to him and the woman who was kidnapped."

I groaned. "I get it. But I'm still going to watch out for him. There's something off about him."

"Don't get too close," the detective said. "Just keep your distance for now, okay?"

"All right. I will." I hung up and tried to eat. I knew I needed nourishment, but I'd lost my appetite.

After pushing the food around my plate for several more minutes, I finally picked up my tray, deposited it in the receptacle, and pushed through the door. I was halfway up the stairs when my phone buzzed. It was a text from Benny.

"I'm on the plane back to Seattle and am about to put my phone in airplane mode," he texted.

"Did you have a good day?" I texted back, while nearly tripping on a stair.

"Yes. But I had a weird vision. Promise me you'll watch out for Braydon."

"What?" My adrenaline kicked in, making my breath quick and shallow.

"What about Braydon?" I sent another text before Benny could reply.

"Be careful," he texted back. "We're taking off. I have to go."

I sent two more texts asking for more information, but Benny had already signed off.

\*\*\*

I was alone in our room. Cassandra was still out with Duncan, and I had no idea when she'd be back. I wished I had someone to talk to. Detective Caruso would shut me down. There were rules he had to follow. He didn't want to discuss my suspicions about Braydon.

I tossed and turned, trying to make my mind stop spinning. Benny thought Braydon was dangerous. It was strangely validating to know he agreed. I needed to discuss this with Benny, but he and Frank wouldn't be landing in Seattle until the middle of the night.

Knowing that I had to get up early for class, I finally convinced my brain to turn off and let me sleep.

*Charity struggled, but the duct tape held nicely.*

*"There, there, my darling. Don't be upset. You're about to begin the life you were destined to live."*

*She grunted and stomped on my foot. A burst of pain shot through my toes.*

*Anger surged within me like lightning.*

*"No," I said with clenched teeth. "Submit yourselves, then, to God. Resist the devil, and he will flee from you. James 4:7."*

*Her scream leaked through the tape covering her mouth.*

*"Shhh," I hissed in her ear. "I do not permit a woman to teach or to exercise authority over a man; rather, she is to remain quiet. Timothy 2:12."*

*She struggled fiercely, and I tightened my hold on her arms. "Soon, you will understand that fate and the will of God is your destiny."*

*With one last attempt to free herself, she wrenched away from my grip and ran into the dark alley.*

*"No!" I ran after her.*

*When she tripped over a loose brick, I knew she'd be mine once again. I knelt down beside her. Her cries were muffled behind the tape.*

*"There, there." I patted her back gently. "And if I go and prepare a place for you, I will come again and will take you to myself, that where I am you may be also. John 14:3."*

180

I sat up in bed, gasping for air. Hot tears streamed down my cheeks. Where was he taking her? What was he planning to do?

# Chapter 27

The alarm went off too soon. I noticed that Cassandra's bed was still made. She hadn't come home last night. I'd have to grill her about that later.

I methodically set about getting ready for class. Before I headed out the door, I called Detective Caruso to tell him about my dream.

"So, he's a religious fanatic?" the detective said.

"I guess you could call him that. He seemed to spout off bible verses to justify what he was doing to Charity."

He groaned. "People like him give religion a bad name. Sadly, others will point to that as an excuse to paint all religion as fanatical poison."

"Are you religious, Detective?"

"I'm Italian, so yes. We're Catholics. From a young age, I've been attending church with my parents and siblings. It's such a part of who I am, that I can't imagine life without it. My wife and I are raising our kids the same way. It's a steady and comforting aspect of our lives."

"That's good." I closed the door to my dorm room behind me and locked it.

"How about you?" he asked.

"My family doesn't attend church, except for the occasional Christmas Eve service. I guess I'm more spiritual than religious." I slung my bag over my shoulder and headed down the stairs. "After everything I've seen and experienced, there's no question in my mind that there's a higher power. I've fought alongside angels enough times to know that."

There was a long pause. I inwardly cringed. Had I said too much? He was probably going to write me off as a crazy person.

"You've fought alongside angels?"

I cleared my throat. "That's a story for another time, but yes."

Another pause. "All right, then. I'm looking forward to hearing that one. In the meantime, please let me know if you have any other visions about this man and where he's taken Charity."

"I will." I reached the sidewalk and headed toward my first class. The sky was overcast with a few patches of blue making random appearances between puffs of white. There was a light breeze, carrying the scent of exhaust from the many cars crawling down city streets.

Walking briskly, I caught a glimpse of Braydon, who'd disappeared into the building ahead of me. Goosebumps prickled my skin. Was he the kidnapper? Could he be the religious zealot who abused his convictions to hurt women?

Though I didn't want to engage with Braydon at all, I still had to attend classes with him. If I could get him to talk about his beliefs, maybe I could determine if he truly was the suspect.

I took the elevator up to the fourth floor where my acting class was located. Students were trickling in, still groggy after a weekend of late night parties or binge-watching their favorite television series.

Normally, I would sit as far away from Braydon as I could. But today, I needed answers. When I entered the large rehearsal room with chairs lined up along one wall, I spotted Braydon at the far end. I took a deep breath and with all the confidence I could gather, I walked across the room and sat down next to him. Despite my newfound courage, my hands shook as I took my rehearsal bag off my shoulder. "Well, well, well." A sly grin spread across his bearded face. "If it isn't Jenny Crumb."

I fought hard to shove down my feelings of revulsion. I tried to act casual. "Hey, Braydon."

He glanced at the empty chairs along the wall and grinned as he realized I'd purposefully sat next to him. "How you doin'?"

"Doing well. How was your weekend? Did you do anything fun?" I attempted some small talk. How could I fit in my questions about his beliefs without raising alarm? If he was the kidnapper, questions about religion could tip him off that I was on to him.

He appraised me with a smug smile. "I'm glad you're interested in my life. I knew you'd come around."

O...kay. I was beginning to question my judgment. Maybe this was a bad idea. "As a friend, sure. I'm interested in how your weekend was. Did you do anything interesting on Sunday?"

He furrowed his brows. "On Sunday? Not really. Just the usual."

What was the usual? Was it "usual" to follow Mike and me to the Port Authority bus station? Had he attended a cult service? Or gone to some fanatical group's sacrificial ritual?

I knew I should reach out and touch his hand—to tune in and read him. But there was no way I could do it. He'd take that as a sign I was into him.

Instead, I continued to ply him with questions. Maybe he would slip and tell me what I needed to know. "So, just working on music for your masterclass or memorizing lines for our scene?"

"Something like that." He winked at me.

What did that mean?

184

Most of the students had arrived and taken a seat along the drab, gray wall.

Randy, our acting prof, clapped his hands. "Let's get started."

\*\*\*

As I walked down the hall to my next class, I thought through my interaction with Braydon. I'd learned nothing about his whereabouts during the weekend. I figured he'd spent much of his time stalking my friends and me, but I had no clue if he'd attended some sort of church. But then again, maybe fanatics didn't attend church. Maybe churches were too normal for people with extremist views.

My mind was swirling with questions, weighing each possibility as it flitted through my head. Suddenly, I realized my mind had been so preoccupied with questioning Braydon, I'd forgotten to ask Benny about his warning text.

I scooted toward the wall to let students pass me and texted him. "What did you mean when you said to watch out for Braydon? Did you have a vision?"

Though the message had been delivered, it hadn't been read. I sighed and continued down the hall.

\*\*\*

After my last class, I rushed back to my room. I needed to talk to somebody. Hoping that Cassandra was back, I threw open the door only to be met by an empty room.

A note lay on my bed. It read, "Sorry to miss you! Duncan came to some of my classes, and we're going to spend the afternoon and evening together. See you tomorrow!"

I sighed and plunked down on my bed. Now that Mike and Benny had left town, Duncan had a hotel room to himself. Feeling alone, I texted Mike. He, like Benny and

Cassandra, seemed to have better things to do. Everyone was so busy.

Knowing that I needed to start acting like an adult and stop relying on everyone else to talk things over with, I decided to finish the assignments I'd been putting off. Then, I would get some dinner and go find an empty practice room in the music building to rehearse for the next day's voice lesson.

When I'd finished my character study homework, I headed downstairs. The cafeteria was filling up quickly. I got some soup and a salad and found a small table near the window. A light rain misted the glass, reminding me of home in Seattle. I watched students rush inside to get out of the rain. Sipping my water, I checked my phone for messages. Still no indication that either Benny or Mike had read my texts.

I scrolled through my favorite social media apps, then shoved my phone back into my pocket. It was getting late. I finished eating and escaped out the door into the early evening's misty glow.

Clouds overhead moved swiftly along the dusky sky. The rain had stopped for the moment. I shivered and wished I'd thought to wear a jacket instead of a hoodie.

Traffic was snarled, even toward the very end of rush hour. Was there such a thing as "rush hour" in New York City? I laughed, thinking that it should be called "rush hours" if it was meant to be accurate.

The smell of rain pooling on the dark pavement rose like steam. A street vendor selling hot dogs was packing up his cart. The aroma of overcooked meat followed behind him as he wheeled his cart along the sidewalk.

When I reached the music building, I opened the door and checked behind me. What if Braydon had been following me and I hadn't noticed? No one was behind me, however, so I walked along the hallway, looking for an empty practice room.

The familiar sounds of singers, flutes, and other musical instruments drifting through the closed doors of the practice rooms gave me a feeling of well-being and comfort. I slid into an empty one and shut the door behind me.

The practice rooms were only about eight by eight feet with just enough room for a person, a music stand, a chair, and an electronic keyboard.

I got out the music I'd been working on and arranged it on the stand.

First, I ran through my vocal warmups, and when my voice felt sufficiently pliant and warm, I jumped into singing. My voice teacher had given me advice for each phrase, and I worked methodically through his notes to make the piece better.

Later, when I was confident I knew the music well enough to get through my voice lesson the next day, I slid the sheet music into a folder and shoved it in my bag.

More time had gone by than I'd realized. The halls were mostly quiet. I could still hear the faint plinking of piano keys in a room somewhere down the hall. I took the elevator down to the first floor and stepped outside. It was darker than I'd imagined.

I checked the time. Surprised to see that it was already after ten o'clock, I headed in the direction of my dorm with quick steps, looking over my shoulder now and then to make sure no one was following me.

Why was I so nervous? I generally wasn't afraid to walk this busy stretch of street alone. There was enough activity and people in the city to make me feel sort of safe at night. But, for some reason, the little hairs on the back of my neck stood straight up.

I walked faster, nearly breaking into a run. Spotting Washington Square Park up ahead, I breathed a momentary sigh of relief. I was almost home.

Ahead, the broad figure of a man stopped, just in front of the taped-off area of the street. In the dark, I couldn't see his facial features. But a sinking feeling was beginning to blossom in my gut. He turned his head both ways, as if checking to see that no one was watching.

I darted into the doorway of an apartment building and peeked my head around the frame of the opening. He ducked under the bright yellow caution tape surrounding the opening in the street under construction. The same street that my friends and I had ventured underneath to discover the coffins and bones.

Just before he disappeared underneath, the streetlight caught his face. It was Braydon Dudek.

My breath caught in my throat. Frantically, I got out my phone and called Detective Caruso. His phone rang six times before it went to voice mail.

"Detective, it's Jenny. I just saw Braydon Dudek go into the opening below street level—the same place where we found the coffins and the bones. Get here as fast as you can. I'm going after him."

# Chapter 28

Next, I texted Cassandra to let her know what was going on in case something happened to me.

I waited for a moment to see if she'd respond, but the message remained unread.

Staring at the yellow tape, I tried to muster up the courage to follow Braydon down the hole. If he'd captured those women, I needed to know where, so I could tell the police.

Before I approached the cordoned off area, I checked my phone one last time to see if Detective Caruso had called. No text from Cassandra either.

Just for safety, I sent a text to Benny, telling him I was going back underground to follow Braydon. If anything happened to me, I wanted at least a few people to know where to look.

Benny replied right away. "What? Don't go down there!" he texted.

"I have to. I need to see if he has those women. You're the one who told me to watch out for Braydon."

"I only had a bad feeling. I didn't say he was the bad guy."

"What does that mean?" I texted back.

"I just had a weird feeling that something bad was associated with Braydon. I don't know what it is, but it's bad. Don't go after him, okay?"

Before I could respond, the street light closest to me flickered.

"Jenny? Promise me."

The wind ruffled my hair. I shivered with a sudden chill that made me want to huddle into the warmth of my thin hoodie. I shifted the strap of my rehearsal bag on my shoulder.

"Hang on," I texted Benny.

"Wait. What's going on?" he replied.

With a sudden gust of wind, Rose appeared in front of me, her dark skirt rustling in the breeze. So, she hadn't crossed over with the other ghosts. There must've been a reason why she'd stayed here among the living.

"Rose is here," I texted.

"What does she want?"

"I don't know. Have to go. If I don't text you in thirty minutes, call Detective Caruso at NYPD."

"Okay."

I texted him the detective's number and shoved the phone into my pocket. I shifted my attention on Rose. She'd moved closer to me, and I could sense the urgency within her.

She turned and pointed to the opening in the street where Braydon had disappeared into and gestured for me to follow.

I watched as she glided away effortlessly, just inches off the sidewalk.

Turning to make sure no one was watching, I followed Rose into the opening under the street. I ducked under the caution tape, stepped down into the hole, and slid through the entry to the subway and into its warm underbelly.

How would I know which way Braydon had gone? And how would I keep myself hidden from view?

190

Rose met me at the beginning of the long tunnel downward. It was pitch black, but her form emitted a soft glow in the darkness.

For extra light, I turned on my cell phone flashlight and followed her as she descended deeper into the bowels beneath the city.

When we reached the place where we found the room containing only the pile of bones, I noticed that police tape had been tacked across the door—and it was slightly ajar. Rose had stopped beside the threshold and solemnly waited for me to look into the room.

Pushing the door open as carefully and silently as I could, I peeked inside to see if Braydon was there. He wasn't, but I caught site of a large footprint in the dust. Was it left behind by his Van's shoe?

Instead of going into the room, I looked further down the tunnel. Rose had already moved ahead. She beckoned for to me to follow.

The drip, drip, drip of water echoed as the tunnel grew warmer. Just as before, the scuttling of a rat somewhere nearby made my skin crawl. Now, though, none of my friends were with me to cling to. I was alone, except for the ghostly woman gliding a few feet ahead.

The tunnel had finally flattened out. I wondered how much time had passed. Glancing at my screen, I realized it had only been ten minutes. Benny would call the police in twenty if I didn't text him first. I hoped Rose and I reached our destination—wherever that was—soon.

I stopped in my tracks. Was that someone crying? I listened and focused my attention on the soft, muffled sobs.

Rose put a finger over her lips. She turned and advanced slowly down the length of the tunnel. I followed, trying not to make a sound as the sobs grew louder.

A large figure moved ahead in the shadows.

"Shh, shh, there now," a man's voice soothed the crying woman. "You are safe with me now. I will provide for you, just like the Lord provides for us all."

My stomach churned. Braydon was a sick individual to use God in this way. Did he really think that what he was doing was right?

I shuddered to think what he would do to that poor woman. I had to stop him. Hurrying, I followed the sound of his voice.

Rose stepped in front of me, as if to keep me from revealing myself to him. She put her hand out in a stop motion. She wanted me to wait.

I stopped and pressed myself against a large wooden pillar. I was so close to the sobbing woman and Braydon. I had to find something to hit him with, so I could get her to safety.

Crouching lower, my eyes searched through the dim light to see if there was a brick or rock to use as a weapon. A dark object lay a few feet away. Was that a rock?

I reached forward, my fingers brushing something soft and warm. The object scurried toward me and scrabbled over my shoe. Stifling a scream, I temporarily lost my balance, falling back on my heels. My left hand hit the dirt behind me, thankfully preventing me from falling further and making noise. I fought to keep my breath measured and remain calm.

Finally, I gathered my wits and crouched forward again. From this vantage I could see something in the dark. A large room or perhaps an abandoned subway platform.

I craned my neck to see more.

Three women were shackled with their backs against a dank, concrete wall. Their arms were stretched out above their heads, their hands dangling loosely from their cuffed wrists.

My breath hitched in my throat. I didn't dare breathe for fear that Braydon would hear me.

He was talking to them in a soothing tone. "There is no need to cry. This is a wonderful beginning for us. Like Adam and Eve in the Garden of Eden."

A keening moan escaped from one of the women. "Please, please! Let us go! We haven't done anything to you. Why are you doing this?"

Braydon cooed and patted the woman's leg. A large column hid him from view, but I could just see his hand resting lightly on her knee.

"It's almost time for us to be united. Let us rejoice and be glad and give him glory! For the wedding of the Lamb has come, and his bride has made herself ready. That's Revelation 19:7."

He was planning a wedding. With all three women?

My mind spun.

"I've brought you each a dress. In white, of course. Your purity deserves nothing less than white."

A rustling sound echoed off the cavernous walls. "One for you, Hope. And you, Faith. Last but not least, one for you, Charity—our long awaited bride. I cannot wait for God to join us in our union."

Another woman began to cry.

"Shh, shh, now. Don't make a fuss. Wait right here while I sterilize the instruments."

Sterilize the instruments? My blood ran cold. This didn't sound good.

I heard his footsteps move away from the women.

This was my chance! If I could figure out a way to get them out of those cuffs, I could get them out before he came back.

Before I moved, I had to think of something I could use to spring them free. My hand felt the back of my head, where my bun was secured with… bobby pins!

I took one out and bent it. Certain it could work, I began to inch forward, away from the safety of my hiding place.

The smell of sweat and fear overpowered me. A large, sweaty palm covered my mouth and pulled me back behind the column I'd been crouched behind. I tried to scream, but the hand tightened, and I was pulled into someone's doughy chest.

I kicked back and tried to jab my elbows into his stomach, but he only tightened his hold on me.

A scratchy beard tickled my bare neck and sent shivers down my spine. Without looking, I knew who'd captured me. Braydon Dudek.

# Chapter 29

"Be quiet!" he hissed in my ear. "Or he'll know we're here."

*He* will know we're here? What was he talking about? Braydon was the only man here—the only one responsible for kidnapping three innocent women.

The sound of humming came from the far corner, beyond where the women were shackled. The tune sounded familiar—I recognized it as an old hymn my grandmother used to sing us to sleep when we stayed overnight at her house.

But that meant... Braydon wasn't the kidnapper. Then who was?

"Promise not to make a sound?" Braydon whispered in my ear.

I nodded, and his fingers moved away from my mouth.

Before the man reached the women, Braydon pushed me toward a hiding place behind an old barrel—one where we could see the man and the three women he'd captured.

The man was about five-foot ten and maybe two-hundred and twenty pounds. He was bald, and his pale skin had a hint of wrinkling at the corners of his eyes. I guessed he was about thirty-five to forty years old, but it was hard to tell in the dim light.

He carried a tray of medical instruments, laid out like you'd see in a TV series set in a hospital. A hint of disinfectant wafted toward me.

Next to the women was a gold-plated basin. I couldn't see what was inside it.

"First, we disrobe and cleanse with hyssop, so that our bodies will be pure as snow." He knelt down and unlocked the shackles of the first woman. "Now, remember. We mustn't resist. There are consequences, as you know." He gave her a stern look.

She had long blond hair tied back in a pony tail and was wearing athletic clothes smudged with dirt. She was the runner I'd seen in my first vision. The one he'd abducted during an early morning workout.

"Hope, my dear. You are the athlete. Your strong body and supple limbs are a shining example of God's handiwork. I am in awe of your strength and beauty. Now, let's get those dirty clothes off," he said in a gentle, almost reverent tone.

My heart nearly stopped. What was he going to do? Rape them? I wanted desperately to check the time. How many minutes had I been down here? Had Benny or Cassandra been able to reach Detective Caruso?

Regardless, I had to do something to stop him. Braydon must've been thinking the same thing, because he too was looking around for something—anything—to hit the man with.

Suddenly, I remembered my gift. Why hadn't I called on the angels for help earlier?

I closed my eyes and pictured an angel that had already saved me numerous times—Archangel Michael. I silently called to him and asked for his help.

Meanwhile, the man had undressed Hope and was washing her body with a cloth and whatever liquid was in the gold basin. My stomach turned. He was a sick, sick individual.

Hope was crying. She seemed exhausted to the point of breaking. My heart swelled with empathy and fear for her. Once he'd finished washing her, he released her from the shackles and dressed her in a white gown, complete with a high neck and long sleeves. She looked like a bride from the early 1900s. He crooned to Hope as he fastened her hair in a bun. "You are perfect. The athleticism and strong body that every woman would love to possess. The first piece of my Trinity."

He refastened the shackles and sat back to admire his work. "Beautiful," he whispered.

Where was Archangel Michael? How could I stop this man?

Next, the man who'd collected women moved on to his next victim. She wore a skirt and a white blouse smudged with dirt. Her brunette hair was cut in a fashionable, long bob—a style I'd seen on many professional women in the city. "Faith, my love. You are the innovator. Your technical know-how and intelligence is coveted by many. Are you ready to begin the rest of your life serving our Lord?"

She let out a little shriek and fruitlessly thrashed against the shackles that bound her to the wall.

"Now, now, angel. You need not struggle. You will only injure yourself if you keep this up. That would be a grave insult to God. Accept your fate as His will."

Faith continued to struggle. The man watched her with an amused smirk. "I will wait until you're done. God rewards his patient flock."

I looked at Braydon. His expression mirrored mine—sheer horror.

Like a car accident, I couldn't take my eyes away from the insanity happening before me. I put my hand over my mouth to keep from crying out.

Faith had exhausted herself. Her head hung low and her shoulders heaved with sobs.

"There." He unbuttoned her blouse and then took off the rest of her clothes.

He washed her with care, singing a hymn in a high and peculiar tone.

I leaned closer to Braydon and whispered as low as I could. "We need to stop him."

He nodded. "I know. We could ambush him."

I glanced at the tray of surgical instruments on the floor next to the man. "He has weapons. We don't."

Once he'd put her back in the metal cuffs, the man moved on to the last woman. "And last, but never least, is my Charity, the healer. You, like Jesus, have the ability to heal the suffering. Your service to His sheep is admirable."

Charity was fighting hard. She tried to kick at him, but he stood just out of reach of her feet.

"You'll soon learn to accept." He put his hands together in a gesture of prayer. "Therefore, get rid of all moral filth and the evil that is so prevalent and humbly accept the word planted in you, which can save you. James 1:21."

He knelt down beside her and took the cloth, dripping, out of the basin. "Let me wash away your sins."

I was crawling out of my skin. If we tried to ambush him, he could just grab one of the sharp instruments next to him and stab us. What if we lured him away by making a noise? My stomach dropped. He was a big man. And clearly deranged. If we attacked him, he could easily injure one or both of us.

"Stay here," Braydon whispered. "I'm going to go get help."

I shook my head. "No. He'll hear you and come after you."

Where was Archangel Michael? I called to him again in my thoughts. "We need help! Please!"

But nothing happened. The angel didn't come to save us like he had before. Was he angry with me?

"I'm going to try to sneak up on him from behind," Braydon whispered. "I'm going to go around until I hit the next platform and circle back. If I can catch him off guard, I can take him down and pin him. I used to be a heavyweight wrestler in middle school."

"Middle school?" I whispered. "That was over four years ago. Are you sure you remember what to do?"

"It's all muscle memory. I'm still in prime condition."

I wanted to roll my eyes. "I don't think it's a good idea."

"You got a better one?" he whispered.

I sighed. "No. But be careful."

He nodded and slunk down the tunnel and disappeared into the darkness.

I never thought I'd want to be in Braydon's presence, but now that he was gone, I wished he hadn't left me here alone.

Was there something I could do while he was sneaking up on the kidnapper?

Then, I remembered my spirit guide, Isla. Could she help me? And where was Rose?

Silently, I asked Isla to come to me—and then Rose as well. I needed all the help I could get.

I stared at the surgical instruments beside the man as he washed Charity. Had he stolen them from the hospital when he'd abducted her? And what was he planning to do with them?

He'd finished pulling the white gown over Charity's head. "Lovely. Just like an angel."

He sat on his heels and admired his work. Three pale, tear-streaked women, with fear and exhaustion dulling their once bright eyes.

Behind the man, I caught a glimpse of movement from the shadows. Braydon moved slowly toward him, trying hard not to make a sound. In his hand, he held what looked like a broken brick.

I held my breath.

The collector stood up. "Now it's my turn to prepare for the ceremony. Thankfully, I had the foresight to bathe in the hyssop beforehand. I have only to put on my robe." He turned his attention to an ornately-carved wooden box. Opening the lid, he took out a white clergy robe and stepped into it. He zipped it up and spread his arms wide, tipping his head back as if he was looking up to heaven. His face radiated joy.

He bent down and reached into the wooden box once more. The collector pulled out a white unity candle, struck a match, and lit it. Holding it in front of him, he said, "Wives, submit to your own husbands, as to the Lord. For the husband is the head of the wife even as Christ is the head of the church, his body, and is himself its Savior. Now as the church submits to Christ, so also wives should submit in everything to their husbands. Husbands, love your wives, as Christ loved the church and gave himself up for her, that he might sanctify her, having cleansed her by the washing of water with the word. Ephesians 5:25-26."

Braydon was inching closer, the broken brick clutched in his right hand.

I prayed that the man was so wrapped up in his own fanaticism that he wouldn't notice Braydon until it was too late.

The collector solemnly recited his vows, then said, "Now we are married in the eyes of God."

He knelt down and picked up a scalpel. "The hands of a healer, the heart of an athlete, and the brains of the innovator. Together, the parts make one. Let us begin."

Oh, no! Was he planning to cut them… apart? My heart raced.

Braydon was now close enough to either throw the brick at the man or lunge forward and hit him. He chose the latter.

The man, scalpel in hand, was swabbing Charity's wrists with alcohol. "This will sting a little," he said in a gentle tone. But even from my hiding place, I could see the light of insanity in his eyes.

Braydon, clearly rattled by what he was about to do, stumbled forward just as the man sliced into Charity's wrist.

"Aaaaah!" Braydon yelled. He swung the brick.

Time slowed. It was as if I was watching a scene from a horror movie in slow motion.

Charity screamed as the scalpel sliced into her skin. The brick slammed into the back of the man's head, the scalpel skittering across the ground and disappearing into a dark corner. He grunted with pain but didn't fall. He turned to see Braydon backtracking.

The collector stood, blood dripping from a cut the brick had made when it made contact with his skull.

Before Braydon could retreat to safety, the man was on him like an angry bull.

"Vengeance is mine, I will repay, says the Lord!" he bellowed. His voice rebounded in the cave-like space. His fists pounded Braydon's face and body.

Oh, my God. I had to do something fast.

I moved my rehearsal bag from my shoulder to the side of the barrel I was hiding behind. My mind raced through scenarios on how to get the kidnapper off Braydon.

Just as I was going to make a move, my spirit guide, Isla materialized before me.

*"Jenny, stop."*

I froze. "Thank God you're here!" I spoke to her inside my head. "Help me!"

She shook her head. *"You have everything you need to stop the madman."*

"What? I do?"

She pointed to my bag. *"Remember what your mother gave you before she went back home."*

I frowned. "What my mother gave me?"

*"You are resourceful. Believe in yourself."* She faded away.

What was in my bag that I could use to stop the collector? Braydon was fighting back. I could hear his grunts and howls as the man hit him. I crouched down and unzipped my rehearsal bag as quietly as I could.

My hand reached inside and felt around for anything that I could use to disable the man. My fingers touched one of my tap shoes. The heel was metal. But was there enough weight to it to do some damage if I hit him?

I didn't think so. Inside one of the interior pockets, my hand skimmed across a cylindrical object. What was that? Suddenly, I remembered. Mom had pressed a canister of pepper spray in my hand and told me to use it if I had to.

This was it. Pulling the canister out, I gave it a good shake and took the safety cap off. I tried steadying my hands. I had only one shot to do this right.

Braydon had stopped crying out. His body was lying in a heap near the sobbing women. The man took a longer surgical knife from the tray and turned his attention toward Braydon's neck.

This was it. I sprang up from my crouched position and surged forward. I shouted as soon as I was within spraying distance from the collector.

My yell took him off guard. He swiveled toward my voice, rage coloring his face a deep red.

He lunged toward me. Was I too close to spray him? I had to be eight feet from the attacker for it to work. Now, he was more like four feet from me.

I tried to spray, but he flew at me and grabbed my arm. The canister sailed out of my hand and bounced. It landed at the feet of Faith, who stared at it with wide eyes.

"What do we have here?" The man had gripped me by both arms. "God has sent you to me for a purpose." He looked up and said, "Heavenly Father. Thank you for your gift. What would you have me do with her?"

I struggled and tried to wrench my body away from him.

But he was strong. His grip never faltered. "Let me hear the word of God!" he bellowed.

Having a vague memory of a video I once saw about self-defense, I brought my knee up into the man's crotch. His grip on me loosened and he bent over, howling in pain.

Faith pushed the pepper spray toward me with her toe. "Get him!" she screeched.

I twisted free and grabbed it off the floor.

Just as he turned his face up to see where I was, my finger plunged down on the sprayer. The stream caught him right in the eyes. He screamed. His hands flew to his face, covering his eyes.

I looked down to see the brick Braydon had used to hit the man with. The edge of it was covered in blood. I knew what I had to do.

Picking it up, I smashed it over his head.

"Umph." He went down and sprawled face first on the ground.

My stomach dropped. Had I killed him?

I watched closely as his breath rose and fell. He was breathing. He was alive.

Braydon, still laying in a heap to the side, moaned.

"Oh my God. Are you all right?" I knelt down beside him.

When he didn't answer, I knew I had to run and get help. The collector could wake up any minute, and then we would've lost any advantage we had.

The women were half sobbing, half cheering with relief. I remembered the bobby pins in my bun and set about picking the locks of their shackles.

One after the other, I stuck a pin in the locks and jiggled until I heard a click. The cuffs sprang loose from their wrists. Once they were all free, I helped them to their feet.

"We've got to get out of here." I helped Charity to her feet, noticing the blood running down her arm.

"Your wrist—it's bleeding bad."

She held her hand over the wound and pressed. "I don't think he sliced through the major artery. But I'll need something to wrap around my wrist to apply pressure."

I rushed over to my rehearsal bag and took out a lightweight t-shirt. "Will this work?" I held it up for her to see.

"It'll do."

I wrapped her wrist tightly with the shirt and tied it into a clumsy knot with her instruction. "I'm glad you're a doctor."

She sighed. "Yes. It comes in handy now and then."

I gave the knot a final tug. "I hope it holds until we get help."

Sounds of running feet echoed off the walls.

April appeared in the gloom of the tunnel. "Jenny?"

I ran to her. "How did you find us?"

"Rose came to me. I was asleep in my room. She woke me up and told me to call the police and then come down here."

Rose materialized beside us. She nodded to me and then disappeared.

Out of the corner of my eye, I noticed that Braydon had opened his eyes and was staring in unmasked horror at the scene before him.

The collector had also regained consciousness. He groaned and raised his head.

My heart caught in my throat.

"April—stand back. He's awake."

She stared at the man lying on the ground, blood running down from the top of his head.

"What happened here?" April whispered.

The man put his hand to his head, staring at the blood in disbelief. "How dare you!" he whined. "God will punish you for this." He attempted to get to his feet.

"Stop!" I shouted. "Or I'll spray you again." I held the pepper spray in front of me. I had no idea if there was any of the substance left in the canister, but I hoped I had enough to do some damage.

He got to his feet, swaying unsteadily.

In the far off distance, police radios blared.

The collector was defiant. "You can do nothing to me. For I am the agent of the Lord. I have the wrath of God on my side. How dare you come between what's mine and God?"

He pointed at me. "The angel of God will smite you with his mighty sword. And I will take my Trinity," he gestured toward the women, "and live as He planned for us to live. The new Adam and Eve—creating a better world in our own Garden of Eden."

Moving in front of the women, I put my arms out as if to shield them from his evil.

The man took a step toward me.

Before I could pepper spray him again, the air wavered. The soft rustling of feathers broke the stillness. Archangel Michael appeared to the left of the man, his sword in hand. He was just as beautiful as I remembered from our adventure in Europe over the summer. Light seemed to be coming from within his perfect form. A soft glow of it shimmered around his body and wings.

April gasped.

The collector's eyes grew huge. "What is this trickery?"

"You use God as an excuse to carry out evil," the archangel said. "This is a grave sin. One which will seal your fate when it is your time to leave this life."

"You are false! You're not real. This girl must've hired you to play the role of an angel. Everyone knows that angels would serve *me* because I am of the Lord. Not some *girl*." He said the word "girl" as if it were a swear word.

Archangel Michael frowned. He spanned his wings to their full extent. He drew his ornate sword, its gleaming blade humming with the power of the Divine.

The collector emitted a strangled cough and cowered before the angel, his hands over his head. "Stop! Don't kill me."

"I will not hurt you." Archangel Michael towered over the sniveling excuse of a man. "Your fate will be determined by justice here on Earth. And your dark soul will be dealt with by God after you reach the end of your mortal life."

Braydon held himself up on one elbow. He watched the angel with awe. "This is incredible."

The angel turned toward him. "Let this be a lesson to you. If you continue to disrespect others and force your will unto them, you will end up like this man. Choose your path carefully."

Braydon flushed a bright red.

I was quite sure that though Braydon had never listened to *me* when I told him to back off, he would heed the angel's warning.

Just as quickly as Archangel Michael had appeared, he was gone in a whoosh of feathers and light.

April rubbed her hand over her face. "What did I just see?"

Realizing the angel had gone, the collector got to his feet. "You ruined everything I've worked for! The hours I spent texting my wives' families, telling them they needed time away. The stupid questions I had to answer to get them to believe it was really their daughters. I lost days of sleep planning for this—preparing for this moment. And you took it from me."

He lunged toward me.

"Stop! Police!" a man's voice called. In the dim light, I could see several police officers with their guns drawn.

"Don't do it," I said in a hushed tone. "If they shoot you, you'll go straight to hell—or wherever people like you go when they die."

A flicker of doubt crossed his face.

"Face down! Hands where we can see them," yelled an officer.

The collector glanced at the police and hesitantly put his hands in the air.

"On the ground!"

I recognized that last voice. It was Detective Caruso. Relief flooded me as the collector obeyed the orders.

A uniformed police woman approached me and the other women. "Let's get you off to the side so they can take him into custody."

"Who's that other guy?" a male officer asked, pointing to Braydon.

"He's a classmate," I answered. "He's been hurt. He'll need an ambulance. And so will they." I motioned toward the women. "This man kidnapped them and held them down here against their will."

April and I watched as the police apprehended the man while Braydon and the three women were taken to get medical help by paramedics.

"That was wild." April looked at me. "You'll have to have to fill me in. What happened before I got here?"

"Later. Let's get through Caruso's questioning. Then you can help me send Rose off to heaven."

# Chapter 30

April and I sat in the chairs facing Caruso's desk. We'd just finished a grueling hour of answering the detective's questions.

"His name is Zebadiah Brubaker. He grew up in a cult-like sect in the Northeast, near Amish country." Detective Caruso referred to his notes. "We're still questioning him. I'm sure there's a lot to learn."

"I thought the Amish are just simple people who want to be left to themselves. I've never heard of them being fanatical," April said.

Detective Caruso shook his head. "They aren't. As I said, he was raised in a cult. They may have had roots in the Amish culture, but they broke off to become a separate community with much more radical beliefs."

A short, stocky officer dressed in blues came in with coffees. He handed one to Caruso. "You ladies want some?"

I didn't want to be rude, so I accepted. "Thanks."

"Sure, I'll take one," April said, reaching for the cup. "Thank you."

He turned his attention toward Caruso. "Horowitz and Mendez are doing the second round of Brubaker's statement. You going in to watch?"

The detective nodded. "I'll be there soon."

"Got it." The officer left.

Caruso continued. "Apparently, Brubaker was institutionalized for a time after his parents died in a fire. He was arrested after police found him wandering the small farm where his parents lived after they left the cult. He'd been babbling about cleansing their sins with the white hot fire of God's wrath, or something like that."

"Creepy. So, he's an arsonist, too." April sipped her coffee and made a face. "Ugh. You drink this stuff every day?"

He smirked. "You get used to it."

I took a tentative sip from the paper cup I held in my hands. Though the warmth of the liquid was comforting, it tasted more like battery acid—or at least what I suspected battery acid tasted like. I resisted the urge to make a face and set the cup down on the detective's desk.

"Can we come with you and watch the interrogation?" I was dying to know how a person could end up like the collector had.

Caruso paused for a moment and then said, "I think that would be all right." He stood up and left the office, waiting for us to follow behind him.

He led us into a dark, carpeted room with a large two-way mirror. The suspect could be watched from this room without being able to see who was watching him.

"This room is sound-proof," Caruso said, taking one of the seats in front of the glass. "But it's best to talk in low tones just in case."

April and I took seats on either side of the detective.

Through the speaker, we could hear Mendez asking, "When did you abduct Hope Becker?"

"I didn't abduct her," the collector said. "She was a gift given to me by God at the end of August."

"Why her? Why not some other woman?" Horowitz asked.

209

Zebadiah smiled. "She was the first piece to my Trinity. Rejoice in hope, be patient in tribulation, be constant in prayer. Romans 12:12."

"You took her because her name is Hope?" Mendez asked.

The man became agitated. "I told you I did not take her! She was given to me. Hope is the athlete. Her strong heart was meant for Trinity."

Mendez leaned back and scratched his head. "Who is this Trinity you keep talking about?"

Zebadiah Brubaker frowned. "The perfect woman, of course. Hope, Faith, and Charity. The version of Eve who didn't take the apple from the snake. The one who obeyed Adam and served him as he deserved to be served. Adam, like me, was created in the image of God. Eve was made from his rib, and she was meant to be his helper."

Horowitz shook his head. "I don't get it. Are you saying you want to marry four women? You captured Hope, Faith, and Charity. But what about Trinity? Were you planning on capturing her?"

Zebadiah slammed his hand down on the table. "Weren't you listening? Trinity is the perfect woman! Made from the best parts of the three given to me by God."

Horowitz paused and glanced at Mendez. "Wait. You wanted the parts of the three women?"

Zebadiah glared at the men and growled. "Perhaps the NYPD needs to raise the bar. You aren't very smart. I told you, those women are really one perfect woman. I have to assemble them—like God would. Perfection is attainable. You only need to listen to Him and understand how that is possible."

I listened with interest and revulsion. "That's why he had those surgical instruments. And why he cut Charity's wrist—he was going to take her hands."

Detective Caruso made a face. "Sick.

April sat stiffly in her chair. "How was he planning on putting the parts together? And what was he going to do with the women once he cut them to pieces?"

The answer came from the collector himself. "Sacrificial fire would remove the sins from the remaining parts. And only the assembled female would be left for me to spend my life with."

Mendez leaned forward. "But she would be dead."

Zebadiah laughed. "No, she wouldn't. Just like Christ lives on though his body has died, so would the woman I built from my own hands." He scowled at the men. "If you hadn't ruined it for me, that is."

Detective Caruso cleared his throat. "I think we've heard enough, don't you? You girls probably need to get back to school. It's been a long night."

He was right. I'd had enough. I didn't want to waste one more moment listening to this awful person talk.

When April and I left the precinct, I checked my phone. I'd turned it off after coming out of the abandoned subway, knowing that I would spend the next hour or more at the police station.

What seemed like a million messages flooded my screen—all from Cassandra, Benny, Mike, and even Frank.

Benny had called Detective Caruso after the thirty minutes had gone by without me messaging him. Cassandra had turned her phone off while she'd been out on a late-night date with Duncan and didn't see my text until well after the collector incident was over.

Her text messages grew more and more frantic as they went on.

I texted them all back. "Everything is okay. I'm with April. We're fine. Tell you more when I get back to campus."

That set off another round of texts from my friends.

"Let me get back to my room first," I texted. "I'll try to answer everything then."

211

I shoved my phone in my rehearsal bag, determined to ignore it while April and I caught a subway train back to school.

*** 

When we got to Washington Square Park, April stopped. "What about Rose?"

I knew exactly what she meant. "We need to help her cross over."

"How do we do that?" April stared at the hanging tree. "She's been here for so long. Will it be hard for her to let go?"

I shrugged. "I don't know."

It was the middle of the night. The city was as quiet as it was going to get. An occasional car drove down the street. A homeless person slept on a park bench nearby. The street lights glowed, illuminating the green leaves of the trees and shrubs.

"Rose?" I stared at the giant tree and scanned the branches for the ghost who'd helped us on numerous occasions.

The street lights flickered.

Rose stood just five feet in front of us, tinted by the light of the nearest lamp.

I smiled at her. "Rose, we want to thank you for everything you've done to help us. You helped stop a madman."

She actually smiled then. The first smile I'd seen from her.

April stepped forward. "I'm so thankful you were here for us. I'm proud you're part of my family."

Rose put her hands over her heart.

"But it's time for you to go now," I said. "You've done everything you were meant to do. You deserve peace."

She nodded.

The soft rustling of feathers drew our attention. It was Archangel Michael.

"Rose." His smile was achingly beautiful. The warm light emanating from him was so full of love, I could hardly bear it. "Will you come with me?"

Her face, lit up by the radiance of the angel, broke into a wide smile. She nodded.

The angel reached for her hand and together they disappeared into a dazzling burst of light.

A white feather drifted lazily down from the night sky and landed on April's shoulder.

I picked it up and handed it to her. "A memento you should hold on to, don't you think?"

April's eyes filled with tears and she hugged me fiercely. "I will never forget this." She turned to head back to her dorm.

"Me neither."

***

When I got back to my dorm room, Cassandra and Duncan were sitting on her bed. Cassandra's eyes were puffy and red.

She sprang up and tackled me, nearly knocking me over. "Oh, my God! You're alive, no thanks to me. I'm a horrible friend. I almost got you killed, and I will do anything I can to make up for it!"

"Whoa, slow down." I hugged her back. "Everything is okay. You didn't do anything wrong."

She stepped back and wiped her face with the back of her hand. "Jenny, I didn't respond to your text until after you'd gotten out of the tunnel."

"That's why I texted Benny, too," I said. "I figured that I'd have a better chance if more than one person knew where I'd gone."

"Did you text Mike?" she asked.

"No. I didn't want to worry him." I felt a tiny twinge of guilt. "But I'm going to tell him everything now."

Cassandra sighed. "I'm so glad you're all right."

She sat back down on her bed and Duncan put his arm around her. "See? I told you all would turn out all right. Jenny's brilliant. That man had no chance up against her."

I smiled. "I had a little help from April, Rose, and Archangel Michael."

Cassandra's eyes widened. "What?"

I pulled out my desk chair and sat down. "I'll explain everything."

"Don't leave a single thing out," she said.

***

After I'd told them the whole story, Cassandra frowned. "You know how you said that Rose crossed over?"

I nodded. "Yeah."

"What about all the people buried in the potter's field? The ones directly under the park, in the dirt? Remember how you kept having visions near the arch? Those people weren't even afforded the burial chamber in the subway. Won't they need to cross over too?"

I paused. I hadn't thought about that. "I guess it depends on if any of them are ghosts. If they all managed to cross over after they died, then they're already there."

"But you kept seeing people in the dirt... right under our feet. Doesn't that mean some of them were left behind?"

I sighed, wishing that I could just go to bed. "Yeah. You're right. We should go make sure no one's soul is trapped."

The three of us went out into the night. Except for the homeless guy sleeping on a bench, we were the only people there.

"Now what?" Cassandra asked.

"Let me see if I can connect with anyone," I said.

I closed my eyes. I allowed myself to reach out my feelers for lost souls. A few minutes went by, but nothing happened.

"Cassandra," I said. "Maybe if we hold hands, we could connect with the spirits better." I glanced at Duncan. "You too."

The three of us held hands. That connection that my spirit guide said would be present between Cassandra and me seemed to open up. I felt a light buzzing in my fingers as they gripped my friends' hands.

Then, suddenly, I felt the presence of people. Felt them gathered around—watching us. I opened my eyes. "Guys, look," I whispered.

Cassandra and Duncan opened their eyes too.

There were at least twenty people standing around us in a circle. Their faces bore the stress, worry, and sadness of the lives they'd lived.

There were old men, young men, women, and children. The children were the ones who broke my heart. They stood alone—without parents. Perhaps they'd died from disease or neglect. I didn't know.

I took a deep breath. "Hello."

Cassandra and Duncan stared. I had a feeling that my agreement with Isla had allowed their ability to see ghosts to become stronger.

The ghosts were dressed in the clothing of their time. Boys in short pants. Girls in tattered dresses. Men and women looking so thin, their clothing swallowed them up— like stick figures wearing potato sacks. The immigrants. The city's poorest of the poor.

"You must be feeling very lost," I said to the people.

They said nothing.

I wanted to hear their stories. I wanted to listen to their sad tales—so that I could tell them to the world and set their words free.

215

But it was selfish to keep them here even a minute longer. I knew I had to release them to heaven—where they belonged.

"Do you see a light?" I motioned around them. "A bright light?"

They looked around at the streetlamps. A little boy pointed to one. "There!"

I smiled. "No, not that kind of light. I'm talking about the kind of light that fills you up with hope. A warm light that makes you feel like home."

A little girl with braids smiled. "I see." She pointed to an area near the arch. "It's getting brighter."

I turned to look. Sure enough, I saw it too. A bright spot that radiated peace and love. "That's it!"

The others, including Cassandra and Duncan, followed the little girl's finger.

"Walk toward that light. You'll be safe. You'll never be alone or scared again. I promise," I said.

The children's eyes lit up. They were the first to run toward the arch. The first ones who disappeared in a haze of sparkling light.

When they were gone, the others followed. And one by one, they were free.

# Chapter 31

After class on Monday evening, I slipped out of my dorm building and avoided the section of the street now surrounded by news vans and cameras.

The media had learned of the three kidnappings and the incident which had gotten the collector arrested. They'd also discovered there were three NYU students involved, and one was in the hospital.

Television news crews and newspaper reporters were doggedly finding out as many details as they could.

April was smart and had holed herself up in her room after her classes.

But there was just one more thing I needed to do before I could put it all behind me.

I tugged my Seattle Mariners baseball cap low to cover my face and hoped the police hadn't shared my name with the media. Just in case, though, I went around the block instead of walking past the media zoo.

A light rain drizzled the streets, and I had to fight to keep from getting bumped by the umbrellas New Yorkers were so fond of carrying. The sidewalks were bustling with people, as usual. There was an icy bite to the rain, and I realized that I'd be cold until spring arrived after winter break.

I found the next subway entrance and took a train to the hospital.

Once I made it to the lobby, I realized I didn't know what floor or room Braydon was in. I texted Detective Caruso and asked if he knew.

"He's in room 202," he texted back. "He's in stable condition."

"Thanks," I replied.

I pushed the elevator button for the second floor and only had to endure a few seconds of bad music. The bell dinged, the doors opened, and I stepped into the hall. The hallway was mostly quiet, except for the hushed tones of nurses talking.

A sign displaying the room numbers with an arrow was on the wall. I headed left. Room 202 was not far.

When I reached the doorway, I paused. My past dislike of Braydon was making me hesitate. But, no. I had to do this. I stepped into the room.

Braydon was flicking through channels of the hospital TV with a bored expression on his face. When he saw me, he turned it off. His head was bandaged, and he had a heartbeat monitor attached to the index finger of his right hand.

"Jenny! What are you doing here?"

"I came to visit you, obviously." I tried to laugh, but I knew bad acting when I heard it—especially when it came from me.

He motioned toward a chair near his bed. "Have a seat."

I sat down and put my purse on the floor between my feet. "How are you feeling?"

He shrugged. "Okay, I guess. It could be worse."

"Honestly, I thought he was going to kill you," I said. "I'm glad he didn't. You were very brave to do what you did. You risked your life to save those women."

Braydon leaned back against his pillows. "Thanks. I wasn't sure I'd live through it either. That guy was really evil."

I nodded. "Agreed. Did they tell you he's in jail? His arraignment is tomorrow morning."

"Good. I hope they throw the book at him."

"Me too. He's pretty unapologetic. I don't think the judge will like that."

"What happened to those women—the ones he had locked up?" he asked.

"Detective Caruso said they would be all right. They didn't have a lot of physical injuries, but I bet they'll have PTSD for a long, long time. I hope they get help for that." Just thinking about them made me sad. But thankfully, they all had families who cared about them, so that was something at least.

"When are they discharging you from the hospital?" I asked.

"In a day or two, I think. I have several broken ribs where he kicked me. And swelling on the back of my head where he hit me. But none of it is life threatening."

"Are your parents coming down to see you?"

He made a face. "Probably not."

I sighed. Something wasn't quite right with his family, but I wasn't going to upset him by asking more questions. I bent over and unzipped my purse. I pulled out a little black box and handed it to him. "Here. I got you something."

He raised his eyebrows. "You did?"

I tipped my chin toward the gift. "Open it."

He lifted the top off the box and took out the silver medallion and chain I'd purchased in the St. Patrick's cathedral gift shop. "A necklace?"

Braydon studied the wings engraved in the middle and the words etched around the edges. "Archangel Michael. Protect us."

Braydon's cheeks flushed. "Thank you. What the angel told me in that tunnel… the way I treat people… especially you. I just. I just want to say I'm sorry. It was an eye-opening moment for me."

I nodded. "Thank you. I know. Nothing I said to you before got through. But I think Archangel Michael's message rang true. He did you a favor by telling you the truth."

"Yes. He did. I see now how I must've made you uncomfortable." He closed his eyes for a moment. When he opened them again he said, "I'm the eighth kid in my family—the baby. My siblings are all super smart. I have to fight to be heard in that bunch. By the time I have a chance to give my opinion on anything, everyone else has moved on and won't listen to a word I say."

I was silent and waited for him to continue.

"So, it's not an excuse, but I guess it somewhat explains how I've treated you and others. At some point I decided that if I want opportunities, I won't wait for them to come to me. I take them. When you sat next to me during orientation, I liked you. Girls don't give me the time of day back home. I made a conscious decision to take what I wanted. I didn't even consider how you felt. And for that, I'm truly sorry."

I wasn't one hundred percent sure I bought his explanation, but it was a start. I stood up. "Thank you for the apology. Promise me something." I put my purse over my shoulder.

"Anything," he said.

"That you'll treat everyone—especially women—with respect. Be humble. Be kind. Don't force yourself on those who aren't interested in either a friendship or a relationship. If you can do that, people will like you back."

He swallowed. "Okay."

"Good. I'll see you in class?" I walked toward the door.

"Yeah. See you in class."

I left the building feeling good. I hadn't let him off the hook. I'd been honest, but kind. I hoped that Archangel Michael would approve.

***

*Two weeks later.*

The bus pulled into the Ithaca station. I caught sight of Mike waiting on the sidewalk. I grinned and waved through the window.

His smile melted my heart. He waved back and walked toward the bus.

I grabbed my purse and duffle and rushed to get off.

"Thanks," I said to the driver.

"Have a nice day, miss," he said.

"I will." I ran to Mike and threw my arms around him.

It would indeed be a nice day.


The End

## About the Author

Martina Dalton writes mysteries and lives in the Pacific Northwest with her family. Born and raised in Alaska, she can nimbly catch a fish, dress for rain, and know what to do when encountering a grizzly bear. Now living in the Seattle area, she uses those same skills to navigate through rush-hour traffic.

**Other books in *The Jenny Crumb Series***
The Third Eye of Jenny Crumb
The Sixth Sense of Jenny Crumb
The Nine Lives of Jenny Crumb
The Witching Hour: Jenny Crumb
Jenny Crumb and the Twelve Days of Christmas

www.ingramcontent.com/pod-product-compliance
Lightning Source LLC
Chambersburg PA
CBHW072234170626
46813CB00003B/1223